"Stop looking so innocent."

Glenn's face was hard as he continued. "Don't pretend that you didn't know about Gran's will."

Hurt flared up in Aline. "I'm tired of being called a gold digger. I've explained over and over that I never—"

He interrupted harshly. "She didn't just leave you a couple of thousand dollars or a piece of jewelry, but an expensive unit in the best part of Melbourne, shares worth a fortune and a large sum of money to go with it."

Aline looked at him in astonishment as he went on. "We wouldn't have begrudged you a nice little something. As it is, I'll fight you. It will cost me more in lawyer's fees than you're worth, but I'll do it and like it."

Only the sound of his receding footsteps penetrated Aline's frozen numbness. Why couldn't he see how wrong he was about her?

Eve Myers is a new author in Harlequin Romances.
In this novel she uses the background of her
homeland, Australia, for her story.

Blissful
Reality
Eve Myers

Harlequin Books

TORONTO • NEW YORK • LONDON
AMSTERDAM • PARIS • SYDNEY • HAMBURG
STOCKHOLM • ATHENS • TOKYO • MILAN

Original hardcover edition published in 1987
by Mills & Boon Limited

ISBN 0-373-17018-1

Harlequin Romance first edition July 1988

CHAPTER ONE

ALINE woke with a start and stared around her at the cast-iron railings of the balcony, the small table with its coffee cup and the long chair on which she was lying. This strange place was a far cry from the nurses' hostel in London and the homes of her relations. It was entrancing, beautiful with an exotic beauty that tugged at her heartstrings and set dreams ablaze. The sampans around the quay were reminders of an earlier age and their yellow oil-flame lamps twinkled like a million stars. From somewhere in her dream, she had heard Jim's voice. 'Hong Kong for our honeymoon? Don't be crazy! Who'd want to go there? Nothing but over-crowded buildings and bad sanitation. Give me the Riviera any time!'

But that was now all over. She had finished with Jim once and for all. He had gone right out of her life and she was going to try hard not to think of him at all, however hard that would be. She knew only too well that many people would say she had been a fool to throw up her nursery nurse training halfway through and hare off to Melbourne. Had her godmother's letter from Australia come at any other time, she might have thought matters over carefully, perhaps postponed emigration until she was qualified. But what girl placed as she had been could have refused just then Gloria Jennings' loving offer of a home and a nice job in one of her antiques boutiques and a new life? Once Jim's engagement to another girl became generally known there would have been much sympathy but also some sniggers, and she did not want either. She had carried her head high, had waved Aunt Gloria's letter at her friends, and here she was now, in Hong Kong, and would soon be in Australia, the fabulous land which had never seemed quite real to her.

So it now lay behind her—Jim and Jim's engagement to a leading cardiologist's daughter, their wedding plans, the tittle-tattle already even among the few who knew all the details, or thought they did, about Jim's and Melissa's appearance at the Hospital Ball and the fear that others might suspect that he had already planned all this while still ostensibly being in love with Aline.

The phone rang. She got to her feet and walked into the most luxurious room she had ever been in. She had never stayed in a luxury hotel before, because her holidays had been spent at youth hostels or at tiny inns on walking tours with her friends, or sometimes even in tents, while hiking. But Mrs Jennings had insisted on this stopover, because she wanted her to have a chance to see one of the loveliest cities in the world.

It was eleven o'clock and she did not know anyone in Hong Kong. She wondered who could be ringing her at this hour. The switchboard operator's drawl told her Melbourne was calling. She had a momentary thought that it must be Aunt Gloria herself, ringing to welcome her.

But it was not Aunt Gloria's Scottish burr which came across the wires. The voice was very clipped, very deep, and did not sound at all friendly. 'Miss Mellan—Miss Aline Mellan? This is Glenn Jennings. I tried to get you earlier on, but you were out.' He stopped and gave the impression that he was awaiting her excuses, but Aline saw no reason why she should have to apologise.

'Who are you and what do you want?' she asked coolly.

He ignored that. Obviously he was not ringing her for the sake of extending a welcome. He crisped, 'Never mind—no reason why you shouldn't have been out. I'm ringing you to advise you to convert your ticket to Melbourne into a return flight to London, the sooner the better. Unfortunately circumstances here have changed and you'll certainly find things strange here, have trouble in getting a job and in settling in. After all, Melbourne is not just an extension of London. If—well, if my grandmother were here, it would be different, but as things are—— Look, Miss Mellan, we're all at sixes and sevens, but let me advise you strongly and in your own interest to do as I ask without asking too many questions. Please return to London. Now. I'll write to you there, or my solicitor will. We'll make up to you for any salary loss you've incurred and we'll do something in addition for you financially, and you can rely on us being generous. I'm sorry, but this is a most expensive call and I'll have to finish.'

What was the man talking about? Aline couldn't make head or tail of it for a moment. Mrs Jennings had wanted her to come over. Two years ago she had mentioned it for the first time, but then Aline had not been interested. Mrs Jennings had brought it up again several time. The last time she had written, 'I'm not young any more, as you know, Linny, and your mother and I were the best of friends over so many years, even although I was much the older. I should love to have you with me. There's plenty of room in the apartment and I shall introduce you to all my friends, and you'll have a lovely time—trips, picnics, dances, and I'll buy you all the frocks and furbelows you can use. Excuse the old-fashioned expression. So do come, and you'll do me a favour.'

Aunt Gloria was not the sort of woman who acted on the spur of the moment, nor one who did not mean what she said. Surely she had not gone off on an overseas trip and left Aline herself dangling?

'I don't understand what you're talking about,' Aline said harshly. 'Are you sure you're talking to the right person?'

'I would have thought that even a babe in arms would have known what I mean. There are reasons, Miss Mellan, why you should not come to Melbourne. I realise that this is inconvenient for you. I tried to stop you leaving London. I rang and sent cables, but you'd already left. We—the family and I—will do everything to make it up to you. My grandmother should have had more sense than to guy you into coming. Look, we'll send you a cheque for six thousand dollars, and please accept our apologies. But it's useless coming to Melbourne now. Perhaps in a couple of years for a holiday.' Impatience had thickened the crispness of his voice.

'Mr Jennings, whether you believe me or not, I still don't understand. And I'm not one to change my mind for no reason at all. I'm certainly not going to let your grandmother down when she's expecting me. If she's not well, I can help to nurse her. If she's too ill to receive me, I can go to a boarding house. But she wants me to come and I'm coming,' Aline said firmly.

'Miss Mellan,' the voice went on, 'I didn't want to tell you over the phone, because from what Gran said you were fond of her—in your own manner perhaps, but fond of her still. But you're forcing me to. I'm sorry to have to tell you that Gran died suddenly.'

For a moment Aline could not speak; the shock was too great. She could not believe what the man was saying.

'Was it—was it an accident?' she asked in a whisper.

'It was a heart attack. She'd been advised long ago to take it easy, and retire, but she wouldn't, and when she finally did it was too late. Also once she'd stopped letting herself get het up about the business, she got het up about your coming.' There was bitterness now, a bitterness which came through clearly. 'The funeral was yesterday. So don't expect kindness and patience from me today—I've clear run out of them.'

For a desperate moment Aline thought he had really hung up. For a moment, a desperate moment, she wanted to be back in England, Jim or no Jim, Melissa or no Melissa, job or no job, accommodation or none. She wanted to be among her friends. But sense came to her rescue. How could she afford to return, tail between her legs, with no money and no prospects? Aunt Gloria had wanted to pay her expenses, but she had refused the fare, she had got presents for her and the family, and had only accepted the two days' stay at this Hong Kong hotel. What she had left over would just about pay for a couple of weeks' accommodation and food in London, and how could anyone rely on finding work there in that short time?

She said, and heard her voice in a disembodied way coming from somewhere near the ceiling, where the lovely lustres of the candelabrum shone brightly, 'I shall not return to England. I'm terribly shocked and very sad about Aunt Gloria's death—and I do want to tend my condolences.' There was a snort of impatience. 'But while I realise that this changes much it doesn't deter me from coming to Melbourne. You may object, but other members of your family may think differently.' Suddenly tears were thick in her throat. 'I shall arrive on the very next plane I can get a seat on, and I'll send you a cable.' Then the shock of Aunt Gloria's death overcame her and the tears could no longer be kept back. She put down the receiver and sank into a chair and then down on the carpet.

A clock struck somewhere and a number of smaller ones trilled their accompaniment and echo. Aline rang the receptionist, who promised to do her best to get her a seat on a plane, and soon reported success.

Very soon she was on her way. The stewardesses on the plane were offering food and drinks. Beneath them, cottonwool clouds spread like a soft carpet. The jets screamed loudly in her ears—or was that imagination too? The faces of Jim, of Aunt Gloria and the probable visage of that impossible Glenn swan before her eyes and then mingled, and while still wondering what had caused his hostility before even having met her, Aline fell asleep,

her problems unsolved, and woke to the realisation that Melbourne was one hour ahead
and that she would have to beard Aunt Gloria's relations who were the only people she
knew something of on this continent, so far
from England.

They were told to fasten their seat-belts as
the plane dropped out of the sun-drenched sky.
Aline stumbled to her feet, shook back her hair
and went down the steps, wondering whether
anybody would be there to meet her, whether
she would have to find her own way to Aunt
Gloria's home, whether she would find anyone
there and what she was to do if she did not.

Tullamarine Airport looked very much like
an English airport. There had been something
different about the Oriental stop-overs,
although, of course, the glass and concrete and
the big sparkling jets had been identical. And
it was hot here, very hot for this time of year,
which she knew was early spring in Victoria.
She turned as a brisk voice spoke behind her,
once she had left the immigration authorities.

'Miss Mellan? It is Miss Mellan, isn't it? I'm
Sandra Wheelan, Glenn Jennings' buyer of
china and glass.' The thought came suddenly
to Aline that, despite Glenn's apparent hostility, he had gone out of his way to find her flight

and see that she was met. He could not be quite so harsh as he had sounded.

The girl who stood there was neither especially tall or imposing-looking, but she certainly was not friendly either. She looked rather bored, in her beautiful yellow uncreased dress, her bare sun-tanned arms and blonde hair carelessly piled above a wide forehead, but piled in such a fashion that it shrieked the attention of a first-class coiffeur. Her casual dress was a model, or close to it. Suddenly Aline felt her strawberry-tinted skirt and blouse were limp and looked even cheaper than they were, while her nice white synthetic sandals were ridiculous. She felt hot and embarrassed in front of this elegant stranger.

'Is this all your hand luggage?' demanded the blonde. 'Well, let's get out of here quickly. It's sweltering, but that's Melbourne for you.' She did not ask whether Aline had had a good trip or wanted a drink or any of the other questions which people surrounding them were pouring out to new arrivals. She led the way out to a small dark car and unlocked the door. Hot air poured out in a liquid stream, but she flicked the air-conditioning switch and rapid coolness spread.

Sandra chattered easily, pointing out wide gardens, mentioning with regret that they had had a dry winter, that therefore there was a water shortage and Melbourne was not looking its best. 'We pride ourselves on being the Garden State of Australia,' she said lightly, as if she really did not care, nor was interested in whether Aline was, but just to make conversation. 'You'll be surprised at how brown everything is. We have to hand-water, but I'm glad to say the Jennings' gardens do look better than most.' And then she went on to talk about the Jennings and the Jennings' shops, where she had worked since she left college, and the Jennings' reputation as the best antique dealers. 'Not a big chain of shops, you understand,' she said, 'but very exclusive, and we're opening more, one or two at a time, and of course Glenn has run the place for ever, even though he let his grandmother think *she* did.' Glenn seemed to dominate her conversation. Whatever the blonde woman was not enthusiastic about, she certainly was enthusiastic about him. She was probably in love with him, thought Aline dazedly, as houses and trees flashed by, and wished Sandra would drive a little slower.

'It's glorious here on the freeway—none of that crawling. Goodness, don't tell me you're car-sick? Or going to be?'

Aline said no, she never was, and for a moment the older girl turned her eyes off the wide road where cars whizzed in both directions. For a moment she did what no experienced driver ever ought to do and looked at her companion and not at where she was going. A lorry materialised from a drive-off like a nightmare. Aline could see Sandra's sudden pallor, the lorry driver's screwed-up, horrified face, could feel the scraping of the car side, or at least thought she did. Everything rocked— the car, the seats, her head and even her brain. Somebody was shouting, somebody was screaming, and then there was silence, except for running footsteps, and a traffic policeman's sharply braked motorbike.

Aline clung to the side of her seat, nursing her aching head where she had, seatbelt or no seatbelt, bumped it. She tried to cling on to her consciousness and found herself wondering how Mr High-and-Mighty Glenn could employ such an inefficient driver. And then to her surprise her head cleared and she said yes, thank you, she was all right.

'I'm so sorry,' said Sandra, sugar-sweet, to the policeman. 'Miss Mellan is just off an overseas plane and she turned sick. I was so worried!'

The car finally went on, a deep furrow in the paint on one side. With a squealing of tyres Sandra pulled in at a restaurant, very fresh-looking and spruce. 'We'd better have a meal here,' she said. 'There's not going to be anything at Glenn's and I'm the world's worst and most uninterested cook.'

'I don't want anything,' said Aline. 'I'm not hungry. You go ahead. I'll have a cup of tea, perhaps.'

'You'll have a good meal, whether you like it or not, because I'm not having you pass out on me. Look what's already happened with you nearly doing so! What Glenn will say I don't know. It's the firm's car and all.' Obviously, Aline thought, Sandra was not going to accept any responsibility or censure, even though it was deserved. Aline suddenly wondered what Glenn's reaction would be.

But she did feel better when the car finally turned into a gateway, gay with blossoming wistaria, and pulled up in front of a tall, imposing house. 'Glenn's, not Mrs Jennings,' said

Sandra briefly. 'And I suppose you can walk and aren't going to pull a faint.'

The tall man who lounged in the patio overlooking the garden was handsome and rugged, not as handsome as Jim with his dark film-star looks, but possessing something else which riveted one's attention to his beak of a nose, his deep-set wide eyes vividly blue in his tanned face; something which would make every woman aware of him. Determined to dislike him, for one long moment Aline found herself staring. Something shivered in her heart as she also shivered in the hot sunshine and found herself regarded sardonically. 'Well, not quite what I expected,' he observed coolly. 'Where's your loot, Miss Gold-Digger? Or have you cleverness enough, wiles enough to hide it? In your jewel box? In your bank account?'

Her eyes met his, steady eyes set in a colourless face. 'I don't understand.' she said. One long slender hand with long slender fingers went up to her throat. 'If we could get in from this heat——'

'You should have taken my advice,' he told her, 'for your own sake. If you can't stand even this warmth how will you be able to stand the stinkers around the New Year and later on?'

'She almost passed out in the car, and yet the air-conditioning was on full blast,' Sandra told him. 'And I nearly crashed it.' Her air of faintly satisfied malice was as obvious as the fact that she was head over heels in love with her boss, and it was equally obvious to Aline that the feelings were not reciprocated.

Aline twisted her bracelet watch on one slender wrist. Surely the few trinkets she had received from Mrs Jennings, however lovely and valuable, did not mean that she deserved the title of gold-digger? She ticketed them with one finger on her forehead—one wrist watch, a charm bracelet, some woollies, boxes of chocolates.

'Sit down before you fall down,' snapped Sandra. 'I'm surprised you managed to gt into Australia, with your poor health.'

Aline kept her temper. 'I had no trouble in passing my medical, and you can't know much about nursery nurses if you think that gruelling training is for weaklings. I've travelled for days, have had little sleep and a shock—and now this reception!'

Sandra shrugged her shoulders and busied herself with the cocktail shaker. She lifted an eyebrow at Aline, who shook her head. It was

Glenn who broke the silence. 'Now listen, Miss Mellan—here, have a drink and then let's talk this over reasonably. It's no use getting into a flap, either of us. Have you had anything to eat?'

'On the road,' said Sandra briefly. 'And she pulled an I-don't-want-it, too.'

'And I take it you didn't stand for such nonsense.' His voice sounded sarcastic. 'I sometimes think, Sandra, you would have made an excellent old-fashioned schoolmarm or a slavedriver. Take your choice.' He turned to Aline and thrust a glass into her hand. 'Sherry, medium dry. It will help.'

There was just the soughing of the air-conditioning and then a small pad-pad as a beautiful Siamese cat came daintily across the priceless rugs. He was perfectly shaped, red mask on cream body, reddish points to soft paws. His voice, the hoarse baby-cry of his species, rose questioningly. He nosed the newcomer and then made himself comfortable on her lap. 'Oh, you beauty!' Aline burst out instinctively. She nuzzled her face against him and a feather-soft, feather-light paw gently touched her face.

'Film and cut,' said a sardonic male voice, which was becoming increasingly familiar to

Aline. 'Or perhaps scrap and cut. We have now seen the frail female in a persecuting world. We have seen the soft motherly girl pouring love on to a cat. But can we now see the business woman you really are? Will you please tell me how much money you want to return to England—pronto!'

Aline continued to keep her temper, but with some difficulty. 'Mr Jennings, would you be good enough to tell me why my presence here in Australia bothers you? And what have you against me that makes you call me a gold-digger? I hardly realised that a half-yearly present, one at Christmas, one on my birthday, however generous, qualifies me for that term. Nor did I ask your—your grandmother to sponsor me to come to Australia. It was her idea and I was only too glad to accept. But where in this is any abuse of your grandmother's kindness? Or yours? I'm beginning to wish I hadn't come; do all Australian men behave so boorishly?'

For a brief moment, she thought she saw a glint of humour in his eyes, but she might just as well have pummelled the panelled wall with her empty flat palms as spoken to him. His face did not move a muscle.

'I'm not asking you to return whatever jewels my grandmother sent you, however ill-advised she was to do so. I'm not asking either why and how much she helped your mother financially. I'm not asking you to account for your fare to Melbourne or reimburse that or the money for the first-class hotel you chose to spend your stop-over in Hong Kong. All I want to know is when you're going, and how much you want. Or if you're too bashful or cunning to tell me, I'll tell you what I offer. You may spend one week in Melbourne in my grand-mother's apartment and I'll provide pocket-money. You can sightsee, and I'll even get someone to show you around. Then I'll get your ticket back to London and I'll arrange to have a thousand Australian dollars deposited at any English bank you choose to name. You will then have had a nice trip at our expense, and a good holiday. And while you of course expected to get a lot more, you won't be getting any of my grandmother's jewels, or anything else she had, or receive any other help. Do you understand? And if it doesn't hurt your tender feelings, or even if it does, and I don't know you well enough to know whether I'm misjudging you in this, there's nothing in my grandmoth-er's apartment that you can snitch. All her valuables have been removed, and what's left there we have listed.'

The feel of the cat's fur beneath her hands showed Aline that the kitten—for he was little more—was feeling her tension and that it made him uneasy. One look at the mirror placed across from her showed that she had no colour in her face whatever, except in her deeply-sunken eyes. But her voice was very steady. 'I have no intention of turning tail and running back to England. I'm going to stay here. I'm not your responsibility and I don't claim to be. Nor am I going to be spoken to like this.' She steadied herself again with difficulty. 'It may interest you to know that I've bought my own ticket—your grandmother offered to do so, but I refused. I only let her pay for the hotel in Hong Kong. It was a place of her choice.'

She stood up and walked over to the window and looked out at the wistaria, fairy-like in its early lilac bloom, at palms which shook their frames and their fronds to the warm breath of the wind, on to a lawn which had been touched by drought.

She realised that Glenn must have been speaking, though she had failed to pay any attention. It came through to her now, as she heard him say impatiently, 'All right, you made your point. You haven't got any feelings, but we've brought you out here and I suppose we must give you a chance. Now this is the only thing I'm willing to do. You may stay in my grandmother's apartment for two weeks. We shall be responsible for your expenses for that time. But if you haven't found yourself a job then—and it's not easy—you will return to England. And no tears and no fainting fits will make me change my mind, so you might just as well spare yourself the effort and me the boredom. Although as far as effort is concerned, being the little actress you must be to have pulled the wool so effectively over my grandmother's eyes, it should be no effort to you at all.'

And instead of all the crushing replies she might have made she said coolly, 'I don't faint, whatever she says,' and with a slender hand, and with complete lack of manners she pointed at Sandra, who stifled a yawn.'

CHAPTER TWO

SISTER TUTOR had impressed on her students that if they were faced with a problem they should make a plan, start at the beginning, go to the end and then stop—and while Aline had always considered that a crib from *Alice in Wonderland* she knew Sister Tutor had been right. Therefore, faced with the task of finding a job in a city totally unknown to her, where many other girls with better qualifications and more local knowledge were doing the same, she was determined to list all possible openings and go through them systematically.

While she wanted to go on with her nursing training she was aware that she would have to take whatever she could get, if she could get anything.

The first thing, obviously, to do was to contact all public hospitals, baby homes and orphanages, and hope someone would at least give her an interview, and the second was to search the papers under nurse-trainee or nurse assistant wanted, advertisements perhaps out

of Melbourne. After that, the thing to do was
to approach private employment agencies, if
they did not charge any fees for registration.

She did all three, but she might just as well
have saved herself the trouble and also the
coins she always dropped into an empty glass
jar for each telephone call. She was not going
to be beholden to the wretched Jennings family
for any more than was absolutely necessary.
She could also have saved herself the fares.

She was to find that the Matrons or Chief
Nursing Officers regretted, or at least their sec-
retaries did, that nothing was available. In
some cases there were waiting lists. She did get
a few appointments for an interview, but when
she had to admit that she only had O-levels, she
was told crisply that what was needed was her
A-levels. They also wanted to know why she
had left her training before she had com-
pleted it. One Sister-in-Charge promised to
contact her former Tutor and if the reply was
favourable there might be a place in the next
intake but one in six months. Another said
she might consider her for her next intake of
mothercraft-trainees, but no, indeed there
was nothing available just now.

It seemed to be a case of checkmate.

Nobody wanted an inexperienced salesgirl who was older than sixteen. Nobody wanted a housekeeper who was less than twenty-five, except one gentleman who obviously wanted more than a housekeeper. Nobody wanted a machinist, however skilful, who was not a professional. Nobody wanted an office girl who had not previously worked in an office, even if she was keen to learn. As for tea-ladies, messenger girls, canteen assistant, the same thing applied. Aline was either too young or too old. But the main thing was that there were many experienced girls who were vying for each job.

She drifted around the apartment, hoping for the phone to ring and yet dreading it, in case it was Glenn enquiring how she had fared. She vacuumed and dusted, polished and cleaned, sat staring at the lovely Melbourne skyline, watched television, ran around the corner to the newsagent, waited intently for the mail to come and cudgelled her brains for another idea, as day after day dragged past.

On the tenth day of her wait a letter from England arrived, and when she tore it open with impatient fingers, a newspaper cutting fell out. From it Jim's face smiled at her, his and that of the girl he was engaged to. Aline stared at his smile and hers, at the tilt of his head and the shape of lips which she had felt so often. She looked at the hand which clasped that of the girl, at the soft curtain of hair drifting down to Melissa's shoulders, the big ring on the hand which she held up for the photographer, the pretty dress, wide eyes, the lovely line of chin to brow, and then she dropped letter and cutting on to the floor and went over to the mirror, staring at herself—soft hair too, wide eyes too, but obviously not soft enough, obviously not wide enough, for him.

The telephone shrilled and at the other end there was a voice, the type of confident voice a Chief Nursing Officer's secretary might have. 'Miss Mellan? Miss Aline Mellan?'

She said, 'Yes,' and hoped she had sounded efficient.

'Miss Mellan, I'm so glad to have reached you at last. I've heard so much about you from your dear godmother, but I only learned last night that you were actually staying in her apartment. I don't suppose you know anything about me, but I was one of your godmother's best friends and she often talked to me about your mother and how much she was looking forward to your coming. Now I wonder—I know you young things have always millions of things lined up to do, but if you're free tonight, would you come down to dinner and then accompany me to the ballet? I live in the same block of flats—fifth floor it is, and I should be delighted to have you.'

'I'd love to,' said Aline. 'Only what ought I to wear for the ballet? Is it—is it evening dress?'

'Not at all,' replied the voice, losing its official briskness and becoming friendly. 'Any pretty summer frock, just as you were wearing in the snapshots you sent dear Gloria. Shall we say five forty-five or thereabouts? That will give us nice time to get acquainted and have a meal.'

Aline whirled happily away from the telephone. It had been the first kindliness she had experienced, apart from the stereotyped and professional pleasantness in shops and offices. It also opened the pathway to someone who perhaps would be able to recommend her to a family who needed a nanny. She opened the huge wardrobe which contained her few garments and carefully lifted out the only dress which might be suitable. She did not fool herself that it would be up to Mrs Delamaine's standards, for she had window-shopped in Knightsbridge and Bond Street often enough to know what a model gown should look like, but then Mrs Delamaine would not expect her to own anything expensive. The green dress was simple, with a wide skirt, an embroidered sash and cap sleeves, but the material was lovely. Aline had splurged on that and had spent many off-duty periods sewing it. She held it up against herself, flushed cheeks, shining eyes, not the colourless waif she seemed to have become since Jim had dropped her. She pressed her lips together tightly.

Bother Jim! Oh, bother Jim for whom the dress had been made. Bother Jim who had talked of introducing her to his family. Bother Jim—and bother Glenn. But for all that Aline had a sudden feeling that she would like Glenn to see her as she was now.

She twisted her hair up into a chignon and considered whether to do it that way. She ran a bath and splashed in some of the bath salts she had never touched up to now. She stepped into the bath—and the telephone rang.

Aline made a dive for the white instrument. 'Miss Mellan?' enquired a woman's unknown voice. 'Are you the girl who rang me yesterday about a mother's help job? You did? Well, are you still free? Because it didn't work out with the other girl and I need someone urgently. Can you come straight away?'

The colour whipped into Aline's face. 'I'm sorry, I'm not free this evening, but I could come tomorrow morning, early. As early as you like. And yes, I am still free.'

'Tomorrow is much too late. I need someone to start in the morning, because we're going into the country. If you can't come tonight I'm afraid it's off.'

She thought of Mrs Delamaine's kind invitation, the dinner and the ballet, but surely, she felt, Mrs Delamaine would understand. She could explain to her. And this—this was important. She screwed up her eyes. 'Very well, I'll cancel. And I'll come now.'

Aline noted the address and asked for directions. 'Oh yes, of course, you're the girl from England. New here, aren't you? I quite fancy an English nanny. You haven't got any commitments, have you? Because we spend quite a lot of our time on our property. I'll see you in about an hour, then.' The receiver went down.

There was no time for a bath now. Aline dialled Mrs Delamaine's number, having wasted considerable time looking for it in the telephone book and then asking the exchange, but it was unlisted. Fortunately it was in the little book by Mrs Jennings' telephone. 'Mrs Delamaine? It's Aline Mellan. I'm most dreadfully sorry, but I won't be able to come this evening. I don't know quite how to apologise, but I've just had a telephone call making an appointment for a job.' She swallowed.

'A job?' said Mrs Delamaine, distinctly cool. 'At this hour?'

Aline tried to explain.

'It's perfectly all right,' said the crisp voice icily. 'I quite understand.' The line went dead.

Outside thunderclouds were netting the sky and the first drops of rain started to fall. The bus arrived after an eternity of waiting. Aline missed the connecting train and the next one seemed to dawdle. She knew she must not miss out on that job. Whatever happened, she must not miss it. This was a live-in position, in the country, when she loved the country, with board and lodging and a salary. She must get it! Whether she like it or not did not matter; she could always start to look around for something else later on.

The house was built in the Spanish style. There were tricycles and a bicycle on the front lawn; a swing peeped from behind the metal side fence and there was a glimpse of a swimming pool, rigorously fenced in. She had to ring twice before the door opened and the woman—the girl—before her looked at her and said, 'Yes?'

'I'm—I'm Aline Mellan. I've got an appointment.' Something in that stare and voice stiffened her spine.

'Oh yes. You're dreadfully young, aren't you? Do come in.'

The air-conditioning met her with a blast of ice. A small girl peered out from behind a door and toddled back. The television set was going full blast. Her prospective employer sat down and motioned Aline to do so. 'I don't see how you can be a trained nanny,' she observed.

'I'm not. I interrupted my training because I was coming to Australia. But I'm nearly nineteen and experienced with children.'

'I wanted a fully-trained mothercraft nurse—I wouldn't consider anyone else. That's what I understood you are.'

Patiently, Aline said. 'I told you I was only semi-trained. But two small children would certainly not be beyond my scope. And as you're so pressed for time——'

'Well, I must have misunderstood you, then.' Obviously the woman did not believe her. 'But I'm sorry, a girl of nineteen without training or experience is of no use to me. I'll pay your fare, but I simply can't see myself engaging you.'

Aline was outside again, in what was now a raging thunderstorm. She was out in the gleaming street with the streaming rain lashing against the whipping trees, with the fences glimmering white and bronze in the lurid evening light.

And that was that.

Fortunately the water in Mrs Jennings' apartment was always hot, so she got into the bath as soon as she got back. She lay in the steam and the heat and got some of the stiffness out of her limbs. Then she crawled into bed. Perhaps it would be best to accept Glenn's offer, to get back to England and to try there where at least she had acquaintances. Never mind Jim. If she only had a job and a roof over her head she could put up with the ache of having Jim close by, while being separated emotionally from him. The Chief Nursing Officer had been right: she ought not to have been so impetuous. She had been a fool, cutting and running because a love affair had gone wrong.

Well, she'd crawl home with her tail between her legs and hope for the best. You could not do the impossible, especially when there was a deadline to face, and she'd have to be grateful to Glenn for providing that ticket.

But being grateful to the arrogant Glenn was something that stuck in her gullet. She'd try anything, do anything rather than that.

At that moment Aline made up her mind to try the only avenue she had not explored before—she'd go to the Commonwealth Employment Service. Probably she was not entitled to be found a job as she was a new arrival and the Jennings had guaranteed her one, but at least she could try. And if she had breached the terms of her visa, and was going to be expelled from the country, what did it matter? She'd have to go anyhow.

'The C.E.S?' asked the friendly woman whom she had stopped in the street after a fruitless search. 'Well, you go around that corner, see, and then it's within a cooee. Used to be right here, but now they've rebuilt. Big open door—you walk right in.' She smiled encouragingly, hitched her baskets higher and went on her way.

Inside there were plenty of stands with cards advertising jobs on them. Apparently the thing to do was to choose the one that appealed to you and then you went to see one of the people behind the counter, or if you wanted an interview because you had none of the experience demanded, you gave your name and waited your turn. Aline did the last and sat down. The bench was not too uncomfortable. Sunshine, weak, watery and gradually strengthening, came in through the windows and groups of young and not so young people drifted around, making notes, or went over and helped themselves from the tea and coffee machine. The girl next to her sighed gustily. 'Wicked waste of time.'

'What is?' asked Aline, surprised.

'Sitting here and registering. But then you gotta do it or you don't get the dole.' The girl stared at Aline's face. 'You know—the dole. Unemployment benefit. Where are you from?'

'I know what dole means, and I'm from England,' said Aline, confiding more easily in a stranger than she would have done in an acquaintance or friend. 'I've only just arrived, from London.'

'You come here for a working holiday or what?' demanded her neighbour. ''Cause if you have, you better not tell them, or you won't get nothing, not for a holiday. I must say they do try to get you something here, but not what I want. Still, here's hoping.' She trailed over to the coffee machine and came back with two carefully balanced cardboard cups of steaming coffee. 'Here you are—my shout.'

'But I—I simply couldn't!' protested Aline.

'You drink it. You look as if you needed it. And I'm not that far down yet. No skin off my nose, a coupla cups of coffee.'

The coffee was astonishingly good, or perhaps, as the other girl had said, Aline really had needed it. 'Thank you. You're very kind,' she smiled.

The girl giggled. 'Aren't we being formal! I'm from the country and we don't care there. Maybe it's different here. I couldn't wait to come to the big town, and now if it wasn't that I'm kinda ashamed to run back I'd run tomorrow. New chum you are, so you don't know the country. It's a different life there. You know everyone and everyone knows you, only where do you take the jobs from?' She slurped the last of her coffee, aimed the empty container at a waste paper basket and did not miss. 'What about you? Ya been London-raised? I believe it's a lovely place.'

Aline tried to tell the other girl about England, the England the girl was interested in, clothes and discos and crowded street stalls, pushing to the back of her mind the abbeys and museums and ancient buildings that made England and had made it for many centuries past.

'Well, you were a fool to come,' said the girl finally. 'Just for a love affair gone wrong.'

Aline's mouth half-opened.

'Obvious, kid,' laughed the other girl, but goodnaturedly. 'A mouse like you doesn't cut and run for boredom. I would, many others would, but not you. And what I want to know is what happened to the job you was supposed to have, because I know you can't get a permit just like that.'

So Aline told her, mentioning no names, giving no details.

'Doubly a fool,' said the girl. 'Don't ya know ya was born? If them high-and-mighties have brought ya out and guaranteed your job, they has to give it to ya—don't know for how long, but for some months anyhow. So don't squat here, waiting and hoping. Ya ring them or write to them or whatever, but get on with it. Don't ya thank me. No skin off my nose.'

For once Aline lost her temper. The realisation of the last weary days, of tramping around trying to find a job when all the time Glenn was bound to give her one, infuriated her—made her see red. She marched out of the Employment Office, grateful for the Australian's habitual indifference to what others did, even to giving up their place in a queue. She managed to get back in record time, still in a flaming temper. And if Glenn had left coming to see her until next morning, her temper might have cooled off, but as it was he came in not long after she had reached the apartment.

Mrs Delamaine also came to see her.

While she was trying to write to Glenn and finding it hard, the bell went and Mrs Delamaine stood in the entrance to the flat. She was a slight yet imposing person, with grey hair piled high above eyes which were strangely youthful in someone who would not see seventy again, dressed with that stark simplicity which proclaimed an excellent cut. By nature or artifice her eyebrows were round half-moons and her manner as straight as her look.

'I've come to find out all about that tarradiddle on the phone yesterday,' she announced. 'From what Gloria told me you aren't the type of child to break an engagement for a better or more entertaining invitation, and while we all can make mistakes I've known Gloria for decades and she never made one as regards human beings, with the sole exception of her grandson. Now may I come in and can we talk about it like civilised beings? If you don't want me to, say so outright and I'll go. And understand— or try to.'

'It wasn't a tarradiddle!' flared Aline. 'It was the truth. I need a job and I was offered one suddenly. And I didn't get it. And if you don't want to believe me—oh, gracious, I'm sorry, I'm not angry with you and I can understand that you're angry with me, but I couldn't help it. And please do come in. If you would like a cup of coffee I make a good one.'

Mrs Delamaine stalked in.

'What I said was the truth!' Aline told her, unable to keep a touch of temper out of her voice.

'This is really excellent coffee,' stated Mrs Delamaine, refusing to pick up the gauntlet of war and doing so charmingly. 'Tell me, Aline—you don't mind of I call you Aline, do you?—how do you like it here? The Art Gallery? Do you find it up to expectation? Stupid me—you might not even have known about our Art Gallery.'

Aline, who had passed it on the tram, said that she thought it looked nice.

'And the Shrine? Did you like the Shrine?'

Aline said she thought it beautiful. 'All those flowers—such beautiful landscaping!'

'What about the Dandenongs? Have you been for a trip up there? And which of our little townships do you like best? Have you seen any of the local craft exhibitions? They do have some gorgeous stuff there.'

All that Aline knew about the Dandenongs was that they were hills and that they represented the blue smudge on the horizon on a clear day. She said she loved hilly country.

Mrs Delamaine put down her cup so that it jarred in its saucer. 'For crying out, child, where have you been since you arrived in Melbourne, and what have you seen?'

'The inside of employment agencies, of personnel offices and private homes who don't want a nanny, thank you very much,' retorted Aline, and walked over to the window, trying to show only a rigid back to her visitor.

'And why does Gloria's goddaughter have to look for a job as a nanny?' demanded Mrs Delamaine. 'Oh, I know she told me she'd offered you a job, but that was only because you were so independent. She certainly didn't bring you out for that. She wanted a companion, a granddaughter, not a stranger. And she had plans for you—dances, drives, parties. And plans to marry you off—yes, don't dare laugh! In our generation it was done, and we don't change easily. And she even thought you might marry that stuffed arrogant shirt of a Glenn!' She put her hand to her mouth. 'Goodness gracious, child, don't you pay any attention to me—my temper runs away with me.' Over her fingers her eyes watched Aline, like the eyes of a cat over a mousehole, and Aline had the strong impression that the slip was no slip at all.

'Marry Glenn?' she gasped. 'I'd sooner marry a baboon from the zoo!'

It certainly was not a good moment for the key to grate in the lock and Glenn to come in with a girl in tow. The resemblance between the two instantly explained their relationship. 'I've brought my sister to see you, Miss Mellan. Oh!' There was a pause. Aline wondered whether he had heard her remark, but he made no comment. He said, 'Good afternoon, Mrs Delamaine. I didn't realise that you two knew each other.'

'Indeed I feel I've know Aline for a long time,' purred the older woman. 'How do you do, Lisane? Don't stand there as if you were frozen. You certainly gatecrashed into the place as if it were empty. I don't somehow feel your grandmother would have approved of it.'

'The apartment is for all practical purposes empty,' Glenn said. 'I lent it to Miss Mellan for a short time on an emergency basis, I didn't rent or lease it to her.'

'I'm going down now,' said Mrs Delamaine, turning to Aline. 'It was delightful to see you. Come and talk to me any time you like. Now, if you want. I can give you a bed.' Bright, malicious eyes glared at Glenn with unmistakable enjoyment. 'Goodbye, Glenn. I suppose I shall see you again, Lisane.' With superb aplomb she brushed out of the place.

'Another elderly lady tied to your chariot wheel,' jibed Glenn. 'Do you always go in for them? Sort of specialise? Gold-digger, elderly ladies for the use of. Or elderly ladies, gold-diggers for the use of. It might make quite a change to try someone closer to your age. Or would that be loading the dice too heavily?'

Aline picked up the cups, very deliberately stacked them on the small perfect tray with its garland surrounds and eloquently said nothing. Her heart was thudding with pure fury. She looked from one arrogant patrician face to the other.

'Well, termagant or not, Mrs Delamaine doesn't deserve to be taken in and fleeced, and fortunately for her I'm here to prevent it happening. Have you got a job yet, Miss Mellan? If not, you're leaving at the end of the week.'

'I've certainly got a job,' said Aline calmly. 'I've had it for quite a long time.'

'In that case may I know whether you'll force me to put you out of the flat or whether you'll leave peaceably within the next few days?'

'Very peaceably,' said Aline. 'Although many wouldn't. Many would object very much to being led around by the nose and fooled, to be forced to traipse around looking for what you knew they wouldn't get—a job. Many would consider it odd, even sadistic.'

'I don't like rows,' said Lisane, opening her lips for the first time. 'I'll wait downstairs for you, Glenn, in the car.' She slipped out of the room. The door of the apartment banged behind her.

'And what do you mean by that remark, Miss Gold-Digger?' Glenn demanded. Surprisingly enough, he seemed amused. It was a new facet of the High-and-Mighty Glenn, which had not seen before. She licked suddenly dry lips.

'I mean I was too big a new chum to know that your grandmother'—try as she might Aline's voice wobbled—'brought me out here and guaranteed me employment. In these circumstances, like it or not, you as well as I have to make the best of it. I have to work for you and you have to employ me. Like it or not,' she repeated.

He leaned forward, not moving his feet, but she flinched as if he had hit her. His mouth was a straight line and the bones showed lividly through the skin. His face was a mask, of fury, of temper, of devilry. And before she could retreat he had stepped straight up to her, with a soft yet quick movement, and had put his arms around her. She saw his eyes just above hers, for he had his hand beneath her chin and was forcing it up. Two inches from her lips and less was his mouth and she could see the sheen of his skin.

She was powerless. She could feel the hard bones of his hand beneath their covering of equally hard flesh. She could smell the male scent of him, the clean, fresh aroma.

Something clicked in her brain, something made her struggle, try to pull away and then, exhaustedly, stop.

Then he kissed her. His hand slipped down her back and she flinched from the touch and quivered. It might have lasted for a moment or for an eternity, and it did not matter either way. She stumbled back finally when he let her go and he also turned to leave. His voice cut through the sudden silence 'Girls who come for what they can grab must learn to take what they've been asking for. Lesson Number One, Miss Mellan!'

The door closed behind him.

CHAPTER THREE

THE JENNINGS boutique in Brighton was one of the loveliest places Aline had ever seen. It was situated in a wide thoroughfare, shaded by crisp awnings, painted in cream and gold, and had big shop windows, which displayed a variety of sumptuous wares, though not more than one or two of each. Furniture, glass, china, jade, jewellery and knick-knacks of every kind were there, antique and contemporary. The people briskly walking past on their way to other equally distinguished and expensive shops paused to stare, while outside the palms waved their founds, the carefully tended flowers bloomed and from over the housetops came the invigorating fresh tang of the sea.

Inside, there were divisions, each with small tables, and there were comfortable chairs for the customers, so that they could look their fill of the showcases. Aline, who had always lived in very plain surroundings, loved to gaze around her and would have been perfectly happy if it had not been that Glenn was so often in the shop and that Sandra, who was not only buyer but also the manageress, did everything she could to make her life difficult.

After giving Aline 'Lesson Number One', Glenn barely spoke to her and behaved as though Lesson Number One had never taken place. There was never a hint of Lesson Number Two. How much he was aware of her she could not say, but she was uncomfortably conscious of the fact that she herself had become very much aware of him. However, the most it seemed she could expect from him was a polite good morning.

This should have suited her, but for some perverse reason it did not. As for Sandra, nothing Aline did could satisfy her. After her surprise telephone call informing Aline that Mr Jennings wanted her to start in the Brighton shop, Sandra had explained to her that, as she was 'inexperienced', she should watch the other staff members and not spoil a sale by giving inexpert service until she knew what to do. There was plenty for her to do in the meantime, Sandra told her—she could polish the pewter, dust the furniture, clean the silver, and only if absolutely nobody else was available was she to serve customers with small unimportant things such as late Victorian snuff

boxes of the cheaper variety, powder jars of the
same vintage, or Toby jugs. All this had seemed
quite reasonable to Aline, who was only too
relieved to be working again. But then why, she
wondered, did the mangeress continually
badger her? After all, Aline had made a few
sales. Very few of the people she had attended
had walked out without buying anything.
When she was finished with the furniture each
morning it gleamed, and surely Sandra must
know that, with the dust whirling in though the
eternally opening door, the pieces nearest it
must get dusty again. Surely also she must
know that Aline was only too anxious to
please.

But no, either she had brought out too many
articles or too few, either they were the wrong
things, too expensive or not expensive enough
for the client. At one stage Sandra blamed her
for not being friendly enough, and then again
for being too familiar. And all the time Sandra
dinned into her that she was not trying hard
enough.

The other assistants were friendly and unob-
trusively tried to help her, but they were busy
and lacked the time to do much. Jane, the business secretary, especially went out of her way
to ease things for Aline, and after the first cou-

ple of days asked her if she wanted to share a room. 'It's only a two-bedroom place, but it's clean and modern and easy walking distance from here, so you'd save time and fares. We share the housework and the expenses and the cooking, if any.' She had grinned. 'There's a take-away food place nearby and it's a big temptation—too big a temptation, in my opinion!'

Warmed by the friendliness and glad to have this problem off her back, Aline had agreed.

The flat had been far above her expectations, and although it was not cheap she could just afford it. 'Award wages', Sandra had stressed, as if impressing on her that she was not getting any favours and could not expect any.

'Of course,' Aline had replied, wondering why the other girl was so unfriendly.

It was obvious that the manageress had been displeased at having an inexperienced assistant pushed on her, but surely she could see that Aline was eager to learn. Why not help instead of blame?

Aline heard enough about the Jennings family in general and Glenn in particular at the shop, and what she heard, except for some tittle-tattle, was in his favour. He had pensioned off Miss Frank, when her fading sight had made it impossible for her to work, and ensured that she did not have to exist on the old age pension. He always gave a nice present to any girl who got engaged or married or who left for family reasons. He was good about granting time off, not just for doctors' visits and dentists but also occasions such as engagement and wedding parties, and he had paid for the tea lady's eye operation, which probably could have been done most efficiently in a public hospital but which, according to that lady, could only be done successfully by the specialist she had attended for some years. And it was not Glenn who had told the staff that, but the tea lady herself. He was on the committee of a number of charitable organisations. He had often bought antiques which some old and poverty-stricken people had to sell, for far more than they were worth. And even if one discounted three-quarters and more of these tales, the fact remained that he seemed a kindly man—to all except Aline.

Aline wondered why. She also wondered why, if already he was so cool to her, she was so stupid as to think of him so much. Because she did. She told herself that she was not in love with him and never would be. It was simply that he kept on intruding into her thoughts. It was perhaps a situation in which she was trying to replace the vision of Jim with that of the only man she had anything to do with.

'There's a customer waiting, Miss Mellan,' the icy voice of the manageress broke the silence, 'and has been waiting for quite a few minutes.'

Aline stared at her. She had been strictly instructed not to touch silver and the client had demanded silver for a wedding present. She shrugged her shoulders. There was no pleasing Sandra.

'Come and let's get some ice-cream,' said Jane a little while later on, sweeping up and shedding her overall, which she like all the staff wore. 'It's too hot for anything else but a salad, and I'm off salads. If I never see one again it's going to be too soon. Why do we exist on salads in our place?'

The coffee lounge was half empty because they were on late lunch and it was almost two o'clock, which was too late for lunchers and too early for afternoon teas. The murals depicted a tropical scene with swathes of land and swatches of shimmering sea, sparkling and inviting and cool. The usual percolator was behind the counter, but there was nobody interested in it and everybody was going for the various ice-cream sundaes.

'I wish I had your figure,' said Jane enviously. 'Oh, I know I'm slim enough, but with me it's suffering and starvation, but you could eat a box of chocolates every day and it wouldn't do you any harm, I bet. Cool drink? I'm going for one. Bother the calories or kilojoules or whatever.'

'No, thank you,' said Aline, thinking of her slim wallet and that she was not going to be paid until the end of the week. 'I'm not at all thirsty.

'Go on,' urged the other girl. 'It's my shout.'

Aline flushed. 'I really don't want it, thank you.'

Jane returned with two foaming glasses. 'Wanting to or not, you'd better have one. And while I'm not trying to thrust in my oar where it's not wanted and you're not the type to weep on anyone's shoulder, would you mind telling me what you've done to put that chip on dear Glenn's shoulder?'

Aline almost choked over the first mouthful and was grateful that it saved her answering.

'All right,' Jane went on. 'I know when it's a brush-off, and I've asked for it. Mum always says I put my feet into my mouth and then keep them there. But what I have to tell you and what I'm going to is that our beloved Sandra, who's a bitch of the first water, with apologies to bitches, canine ones which I like, is not just nasty because of her loving nature. She's been told to get you out, and boy, is she enjoying herself! She can't stand anyone around her dear darling Glenn, who doesn't even know she exists except as a darn good buyer, which she is. So, if you won't give, and you being a new chum—gosh, how I hate that expression, but what else is there to say?—I'm quite willing to help you and show you the ropes. Firstly, because I like you and secondly because I'd like to black dear Sandra's eyes and pay her out for her nastiness, and mainly because I don't like to see anyone done down, and Glenn is doing you down. As I said, I don't know why, because give the devil his due, and he's a fascinating one, he's got a good relationship with the staff and he's generally a decent bloke.'

A coffee lounge ought not to serve ice-cream which was not edible, without flavour, without sweetness, without tang, and which tasted like lumps of cold nothingness. She'd never come here again, Aline thought. Of course she would never have come here anyhow, because after what she had just heard she was going to quit.

Never mind, she thought, where her next job would be coming from. Never mind everything. She had had it. Her patience had come to an end.

'I'm going to walk out on them,' she decided, and put her spoon down with a tinkling of metal against glass.

'You nuts or something?' said Jane. 'Don't you watch the TV? Or read the papers? Or listen to the wireless or to what people are talking about? Didn't you hear Linda going on about how hard it is for her sister to get a job? Haven't you heard Bridget going on about her sister-in-law, who's a trained teacher and had been running herself ragged for ages before she found something? What hell's chance have you got of getting anything at all? Have some sense, Aline, do! And if you're thinking of the dole, then stop it. I'm not all that up on migrants and what they can or can't do, but I know that if any of us walk out without good and sufficient reason we have to wait for a while. And whether the Commonwealth Employment Service office would consider your reason a good one, I'm sure I don't know. So, as my gran says, don't you dare go pouring out the baby with the bath water!'

'I'm going to leave all the same,' said Aline, but her voice shook.

'You look around for something else, but don't you go off your head. Whether you like Jennings or not, you get a good wage, you can pay your way and put a bit aside, and you're getting experience. Oh, no, just look at the time! We gotta run. If I'm late her ladyship might not open her mouth, depending on how she feels, but with you there, she'll hit the roof. Let's go.'

But Aline did not need to make up her mind whether to leave or not, because the very next day she was sacked.

It had been 'one of those days' right from the beginning. Opening a lazy eye, Jane stared at the clock and almost fell out of bed. 'Aline, Aline, hurry up! It's almost eight-thirty. We'll never make it.' She shook back her mop of black silky hair and moaned. 'And the heat! Is it September or isn't it? And so early in the morning? Who'd live in Melbourne?' She dashed for the bathroom, while Aline slipped into the kitchen to pour some iced fruit juice.

Now Melbourne could be called the weather capital of the world, both approvingly and otherwise. It was a state that, in the midst of winter, could have lovely warm days, with the hardy cold weather flowers a-bloom, while in the midst of summer there were times when the breeze came straight off the sea. Aline had heard somewhere that Melbournians are born with a mac on their shoulders, a sunshade between their teeth and a bikini beneath their sweaters.

This particular day was lifted straight out of the cauldron of boiling misery, with the wind blowing sticky heat on to a gasping world, while the palm fronds drooped and so did the people on trams and buses, in cars and on bikes. Even their skimpy sun-frocks seemed a burden, and neither girl could imagine how they were going to feel inside the very smart tan uniforms Jennings supplied. Jane's grumbles never ceased, while Aline plodded grimly by her side and thought her own thoughts, which were not pleasant.

'Well, there's one thing—it will be cool at Jennings,' said Jane, pushing her hair off her hot forehead.

'The air-conditioning's superb,' agreed Aline, glad to find something cheerful on a day like this.

'I wasn't talking of the temperature but of Miss Bitch, so-called,' snapped Jane. 'One look at her seems enough for me nowadays. Ooops, there we are—one minute to spare, and just look at her glaring!'

Not many customers came in and there were few passers-by. The respite ought to have been welcome, except that Sandra seemed to be possessed more of the devil than usually. She wanted this cleaned, even though it had been cleaned a day ago; she wanted that shifted back to where it had been the week before. The show windows were overloaded; the front shelves were too bare. Aline kept on looking at the door and she fidgeted, something that she never did, when an old and valued customer came in, bringing ice-cream for the girls. Sandra blew up in the privacy of the kitchenette, damning interfering busybodies, while the assistants watched her with interest.

'Dear Glenn's done what she didn't expect him to or didn't do what she wanted,' giggled one girl. 'Doesn't she ever get tired of trying? He doesn't even know she exists, as a female and an attractive one, that is. More fool she!'

'I'm sure I don't know what's got into her lately. I wish she'd get the summer 'flu or heat exhaustion, or get married. Anything as long as she gets out of my hair!' The latest sneaker licked ice-cream off her fingers and said that was exactly what she had needed.

A few clients came in during the afternoon, mostly just fingering the less expensive wares. Then Glenn walked into the shop, going straight through into his office, and a little while later, Sandra told Aline he wanted to see her.

'Here we go again,' muttered Jane to herself, but while she had every intention of standing guard as close to the door as she could, the telephone rang and she had to go into her minute bureau.

Glenn was standing behind his big, beautiful hand-crafted desk, which was a genuine antique. His skin was even more tanned than before, and Aline found herself wondering whether he had spent some time on the beach. Someone—it might have been Jane—had told her that he owned a small boat and often took it out. For a moment she could see him standing there in the spray, with the wind ruffling his hair, a pirate captain directing operations on board his ship in the days of the Spanish Main, cutlass in his teeth and laughter in his eyes, while his corsairs ruffled gaily round him. She pulled herself together sharply and said quite coolly, 'You wished to see me, Mr Jennings?'

'You've been here for over a week now, Miss Mellan. I realise that you're lacking in experience and so does Miss Wheelan, but even a raw novice should have done better than you.' For once his voice was tired, as if the excessive humidity had drained even some of his vitality. 'Miss Wheelan tells me you don't have the makings of a good saleswoman, that you're not even trying. I've looked at your sales record.' He pushed it across the width of the desk towards her. 'I was prepared to instruct Miss Wheelan to have patience, to try once more to teach you and give you another chance, but after seeing this there's nothing I feel I can do.'

Aline stood facing him. Her tan uniform, with its ruffled collar, showed up the pallor of her face. Her eyes were fixed on the drab piece of paper. Words were revolving in her mind. 'But she wouldn't let me try . . . ' she began.

It was as though she had not spoken. His face was impassive. Could Lesson Number One ever have taken place?

'Employing you,' he said, 'is not merely a waste of money, which I might be prepared to stand for a time, but it's also losing us customers, which neither we nor any other business can afford. This is definite, Miss Mellan, and it's no use appealing against my decision.'

Whatever else he meant to say was never going to be said, because like a robot Aline turned and walked out, cutting him off right in the middle of a sentence.

Outside the office door Sandra stood, obviously eavesdropping on the monologue which had been going on. She snapped, 'Miss Mellan, where do you think you're going?' and put out a detaining hand, but Aline pushed past her. One of the other girls asked. 'What's biting you, love? You sick? but Aline could not even muster a mechanical smile. To her left the door to the tiny staff room stood open, and she picked up her bag and turned towards the exit. A blast of hot air met her as she stepped out of the air-conditioned premises, and she had not taken ten steps when Jane came running after her. 'Aline, Aline, come back this moment! You crazy or something?' A big red bus had just drawn up and, desperate, feeling everyone was trying to stop her, Aline swung herself on to it. The conductor asked, 'Where to, love?' and she gave him a blank stare and with a hazy memory of having seen 'Princes Bridge' on it gave that as her destination.

There were few people on the bus, and these looked limp. A couple of women were talking about the furniture sale in one of the city shops. A mother was consoling a crying toddler with the promise of a 'big ice-cream', and a young man was scowling through the window. Thoughts went through her mind—Melbourne, lovely city. Melbourne, friendly city. Well, it was. Her colleagues, the shopkeepers, even most strangers, wore a smile and a genuine one, but for Aline it was a strange one, in a strange continent where she did not know anyone. She closed her eyes tight, thinking of London in the mizzle, London in the drizzle. London on a fine day when the sparrows chirped and the sun gilded the roofs, and the Household Cavalry brought the olden days and their pageantry into modern London.

She wasn't anywhere near Princes Bridge Station, but she saw the silver gleam of the sea, its silver sheen with the frothing dance of the waves. She got off the bus and walked along the shore, until there was only water and parched grass and beautiful sprawling houses in the background. She walked until she could walk no more, then she sat down on a bench and considered the future and its lack of prospects.

She wanted to go back to England. She wanted to be back in England. How was she to do that?

She had to manage somehow without being beholden to Glenn. A sudden vision of Glenn's smile, Glenn's frown, Glenn's arrogance came into her mind. Why should she think about Glenn, who had behaved so boorishly? She had to forget him. She *had* to.

She had read somewhere that if you wanted to get back to England and you had no money, you went to the nearest British Consulate or Embassy and they sent you home as a distressed person. It was something which did not appeal to Aline, yet apart from her homesickness, England was her only chance. There she could stay with one of her relations or friends for a few days, but she did not want to push herself on to them for long, but it would give her a breathing space. She could approach Sister Tutor and confide that Australia had not worked out for her, and Sister Tutor would speak to the Chief Nursing Officer, and even if they could not or would not accept her immediately as a trainee, they might find her a job as a domestic in the Babies' Home. Or she could always find work as a daily. She might not be old enough for a housekeeper, but desperate mothers and business people did not look too closely at the age of a charwoman. And she could live simply. She was not used to luxury, nor had she really hankered after it.

And then she sat bolt upright, right in the middle of the heat-parched vegetation, where everything drowsed limply. Why in her whole search for jobs had she not thought before of being a daily? Here in Australia surely there were also business people, there were mothers, there were elderly people who required some-one once or twice a week, to do their housework. And she could live in a hostel, and save up her money and then return to England. Under her own steam.

The tight band of frustration, of tension and misery in her snapped. Her eyelids drooped lower. There was a small wind playing in the leaves. She dozed off.

Hours later, when she woke, she looked round her dazedly. She knew instantly that it was late, for though it was still very hot the sky was netted with the shadows of approaching dusk. Cars whizzed past and a traffic jam had built up at the crossroads. She looked down at her watch. It couldn't be as late as all that, surely?

She reached out for a handkerchief to wipe the moisture off her forehead and found that her bag was gone. Someone had stolen it while she slept, and she was left with no money, no keys, not as much as a twenty-cent piece which would enable her to ring her flatmates and ask them to come and pick her up.

There was nothing else for her to do but walk home. How far was it? Six miles? Seven? More? She didn't know. It was true that she had crossed and criss-crossed Melbourne in her search for work, but she didn't know it as well as all that. And how would she find her way to Brighton? You couldn't go up to people and enquire, because they would direct you to the nearest tram or bus or station. Nobody in Melbourne walked that far, especially in that heat.

The first part was easy enough. Aline managed to find the main road and followed the tramlines. The air was full of fumes which mingled nauseatingly with the stifling breeze. The tarmac seemed soft beneath her feet. It was fortunate that she had gone in for sport and had experienced almost a year of nurses' training and was used to walking, but this was almost too much. She found Napean Highway at last, but there were many side-roads. She

realised she would have to ask for directions.
But who was there to ask? There were cars,
there were bikes and mopeds and motor-cycles.
Buses panted past, trams jingled, but nobody
walked.

The first person she asked could not help.
'Brighton? Sorry, love, I'm a stranger here
myself. I'd take the next road—you're sure to
find someone there who'll know.'

The next was no more helpful. 'Brighton?
You take the next on your left—well, I'm sure
it's the left. What say, Frank? No, right will get
her into Elwood. Why not take a tram? There's
a stop there, the conductor will know. Sorry.'

The third she asked was definitely off-put-
ting. 'Brighton? What ya wanna walk there for,
chick? Ya come along of me. Have a nice little
drinkie and then we'll see.'

Putting on a spurt, Aline fled.

The long shape of a car pulled up beside her.
'Want a ride, kid? It's too hot to walk.'

You could not outrun a car. Aline looked
straight ahead and went on walking. Beside
her, the car kept up its pace, and she remembered all the horrors from the TV, the wireless
and the newspapers. After a short but endless-
seeming time, the sleek shape of a police vehi-

cle hove into view and with a rush and a roar her persecutor vanished.

'I'm lucky,' thought Aline, trying hard to find something to laugh at, 'that I don't live in Moorabbin or Oakleigh or the even more outlying districts!'

Slowly the streets became familiar. She recognised their usual shopping centre, not the one close to the boutique where everything was more expensive and exclusive, but the one where they shopped on Friday evening and Saturday afternoon. In another five minutes she was dragging herself up the steps, thinking of an icy milk-shake, an ice-cream soda, which for some reason here they called a spider.

She rang the bell and its peal came back to her, then muted into silence. There were no answering footsteps, no door banging, no sound. Obviously her flatmates were out.

Aline sat down on the steps, licking dry lips and thinking longingly of cold water. It was dark now, too dark to see the tiny watch which did not glow at night. It must be very late, she thought. Somewhere in the flats people were quarrelling. Some television sets were going.

She had just decided to go down to the caretaker and ask for a glass of water when she heard footsteps—Jane's footsteps. Aline staggered to her feet. 'Jane—Jane!'

'Aline!' A whirlwind rushed up to her, a pair
of arms was thrown around her neck, as the
usually very reserved Jane cast reserve to the
winds. 'Where have you been? We've all been
looking for you and looking for you. We were
close to going to the police. Do you know the
time? It's close to ten o'clock. We couldn't
imagine where you were. Why aren't you inside
the flat? My gosh, you're hot! Whatever's the
matter, and what made you behave like that?
So dotty! We've all been out of our minds. Even
Sandra was worried.'

'I should see that day,' thought Aline. She
finally got out in what was not much more than
a whisper, 'My handbag—stolen. I walked,
miles and miles. Jane, I must have water. I'm
parched!'

There were lights and there was water. There
was tea and the sharp nip of brandy. And
there—incredibly—was Glenn, bending over
her and holding the glass to her lips. 'Drink,
Miss Mellan. It's on the house.' She wondered
whether she imagined there was a softer note
in his voice.

'No more,' she gasped. 'Thank you.'

'What you need is something to eat and bed,'
bustled Jane, bringing in a tray with scrambled

eggs and a few juicy slices of tomato. 'Light and easy and nourishing. And I didn't make toast because I don't think you could get it down, but try that scone. It's hot.'

'I'm sorry to be giving you all that trouble,' muttered Aline.

'Trouble,' said Glenn staring down at her, his exasperation again leavened with that softer note. 'You vanish in the early afternoon. You rush out and go missing. You don't turn up at the flat. You interrupt the work at the shop and worry the hell out of us. All this when I've arranged for you to go as nursery governess, or nursery nurse, or whatever you like to call it, to my brother Bill on his Queensland property, and that sort of work should be more to your liking—or we hope so. Anyhow, you can't possibly be a worse children's nurse than you've been a sales assistant.'

Before Aline could say she did not want any of his arrangements, Kate, one of her flatmates, advised in her soft Scottish voice, 'Dinna be daft, lassie, and shut up.'

Against her instincts, Aline did remain silent, not pausing to ask herself the reason.

CHAPTER FOUR

GLENN'S instructions to Aline had been explicit. She was to fly to Brisbane where Bill would meet her and escort her to his property, which was close to a small township—'close' in Australian terms meaning miles from any neighbour. She understood that a cousin ran his household and Aline's sole responsibility would be his motherless twins. Glenn had told her what salary she was to receive, and it had seemed princely to her, especially as she was also getting free board and lodging. She realised gratefully that she would be able to repay over a comparatively short period all she owed to the Jennings and then save to go home to England.

Before leaving the flat, Glenn had handed her an envelope, and when next morning Aline opened it, she found not only an air ticket but also a few big notes of money with Glenn's scrawled orders to use it to outfit herself for the heat of Northern Queensland. Aline almost laughed. Surely nothing could be any hotter than this Melbourne so-called spring! And whatever the lordly Glenn decreed, she was not going to plunge any deeper into debt just to buy a few unnecessary frills.

'You're being an idiot,' cautioned Jane. 'After all, it's like uniforms. You didn't make any fuss over wearing the shop overalls, why make a fuss about this? And while it seems a lot of money to us, it's nothing to him. It's really hot up there, so go out and get yourself something. Half your luck—I'd just love to go splurging!'

'You take that money right back to Glenn, Jane, please,' Aline begged, but Jane said she was all for a quiet life and she was not going to beard Glenn, although she would be willing for Aline's sake to beard any lion in his den. 'Glenn has his attractions,' she observed, 'but he can be a bit of a pain at times, and I don't need to tell you that.'

'All right, then. Here's an envelope. Give him that envelope, and you don't need to tell him you know what's inside. As a matter of fact, you don't, so you're not telling him a lie.' Aline wheeled, turning her back on Jane, and stuffed the money into the envelope. 'After all, this just might be a thank-you note of acknowledgement.'

'Sez you,' said Jane sceptically, but she put it into her handbag.

The flat was quiet—heavenly quiet. Aline took a shower, drank first one and then another cup of tea. She looked out of the window at the strip of sea out on the right. There was no doubt that Australia was beautiful, and one day, when circumstances were different, she would come back for a lovely holiday. She'd stay at the Southern Cross Hotel or at the Wentworth. She'd go shopping in George's. She would take a trip right out to Alice Springs and famous Ayers Rock. She would go camping in the Outback and see the marvels of this very new and yet so ancient continent.

A little bubble of pleasure sprang up in her as she realised suddenly that the dream of tomorrow could at least partially become the reality of today, because she was going close to the edge of the Outback. She would see Brisbane and its beaches, Queensland and its lovely wide stretches and maybe its fields of sugar cane. She would meet aborigines and talk to them, and maybe Bill would ignore her and leave her in peace and the twins would love her. They were tinies, after all, and children, however spoiled, were lovable.

Before packing she had everything on her bed, carefully inspecting for loose buttons and straps which were not as secure as they should be, while the washing machine which was part of the flat did most of the work for her. She blinked when the bell rang. What could it be? A telegram? A parcel?

The bell pealed again before she had time to reach the door and with some vague foreboding she opened it.

It was Glenn, dressed in a suit, his open-collar shirt in a deeper shade, and a cream and scarlet silk square in his hand which must have fitted into the collar. He now used it to wipe his face. 'Miss Mellan, do you have to be even more of a fool than usual?' he said, with a deceptive smoothness of voice. 'And waste my time? Although why do I ask? Either you're the worst idiot in the world, which I'm starting to suspect, or the most accomplished actress, which I'm starting to doubt, but whichever way, I've had it with you, and the only consolation I've got is that I'm getting you out of my hair, and I'm seriously thinking of escorting you to the airport tomorrow morning, just to be certain that you catch the plane. I can't believe I'll be that lucky. And the only thing that's making me hesitate is the fear that I'll lose my head and do a wild dance of relief right there and be rushed into the nearest mental hospital by people who don't know you. Anyone who does would dance with me.'

Aline gurgled with laughter.

He stared at her, his face darkening. The high-and-mighty lord of Jennings, the darling of the society pages, the pin-up boy of the sports writers, she thought, would be used to everything from adoring women and admiring males except laughter.

'You're not having hysterics?' he demanded, looking around, whether with the unkind idea of dousing her with water or the more kindly one of restoring her with brandy was uncertain.

'No-oo,' was all that Aline could bring out. 'But the idea of you—oh, Mr Jennings, please, please don't let's scrap. Not today. I—I simply haven't got the strength.'

'*You* haven't? What about me? What about Sandra? What about Jane? You? You may look the little princess out of the pantomime, which is a daft thing to say, but you're the most exasperating girl I've ever had the misfortune to meet, and anyone who's met you and got away remaining sane should get the Nobel Prize for

sheer pure endurance and strength of charac-
ter. Haven't you got any sense? Or intelligence?
Haven't I explained to you that Bill's place is
practically the Outback and your imsy-mimsy
town clothes won't do out there? What do you
want to do? Kill yourself? Or Bill?'

'I just don't need extra clothes. I've got
jeans—I've got sandals. I've got blouses and
cardigans. I've got a mac. I've got sun-frocks.'
Aline squeezed her eyes shut tightly, hoping
that they would not betray her in that grandi-
loquent recital of her few poor bits. 'What else
does one need in that Outback of yours—or of
your brother's? A diving suit?'

'No, seeing that there's only the dam you
could possibly dive into, though you're quite
capable of trying even that nonsense. What you
do need is good stout shoes—there are snakes.
What you also need is something to cover your
head, or do you mean to lock yourself and
those unfortunate kids into the house and stay
there?—and I wouldn't be surprised at that.
Riding clothes, even if you can't sit a horse, and
I don't suppose you can, unless you've done
your stint in—what's it called—Rotten Row?
Have you?'

Aline wondered why she should invariably
lose her temper with Glenn. But this really was

too much. Perhaps he had never been to London, but whether he had or not, didn't he realise that only wealthy people or horse-mad ones went riding in the Park? Didn't he know what it cost to keep a horse? To hire a horse and get the proper outfit?

She managed a 'Yes' and then changed it to 'No', and made it sound mutinous.

'And I suppose your clothes are all man-made fibre material?—that stuff which doesn't breathe? Well, they're all right and even good in cool climates, or so my sister tells me, but you just try to wear them in great heat and see where it gets you. Why do you think you've been looking like a boiled beetroot right along? Because you're loaded up with non-breathe panties and petticoats and whatever else you women wear!'

Aline instantly fired up. 'You're the rudest man in the world, and I don't care if you're my boss, or quasi-boss, and I don't care whether I shouldn't say things like that to you, but I'm not going to be spoken to like—like an idiot!'

She took a step backwards, but she was too late. He was already on his toes, looking like a hungry tiger which had been crossed.

'Don't you dare!' she managed to get out, in such a low whisper that he could not have heard. At least she suddenly hoped that he could not have heard, for she realised she had tossed him a plain dare. The lord of the Jennings empire dared what he wanted.

'Oh no?' he said, very softly, very dangerously, his eyes glinting from narrowed slits, some slight colour beneath his tan. 'Oh no. So I don't dare, Miss Gold-Digger? Is that what you think? Or pretend to think?'

She wanted to run, but where could she go? If she could get to the bathroom there was a bolt, but she did not think she could make it. Obviously Glenn could move quicker than she. Something in her quailed, something else, something strong and warm and feminine, rejoiced, because at last he was seeing her, not as his godmother's protégée, not as a sales assistant who had barged into his shop and whom he had considered useless, but as a person.

'Don't be stupid, Glenn,' she said rashly.

He took no notice. She heard him say, 'You can't have your cake and eat it, my darling little conceited idiot of a gold-digger. So I do dare—like this and like that and . . . '

He had her in his arms and he was holding her at arm's length. He was drawing her closer, very slowly, very gently, yet letting her feel the

iron strength of muscles bunched behind
tanned skin. He was running his lips over her
eyebrows, her closed eyes and her throat. He
was touching the throbbing hollow, the V-neck
of her blouse left bare. And then he was kissing
her in a punishing way, a victor's brute
caresses, harsh warm kisses which drew the life
from her, which left her weak in his embrace.
Harsh kisses that punished even more than they
demanded and which she ought to hate. And
to her horror she found that all the same she
was melting into them, that she was weak and
still and limp and then responding to his kisses,
wanting him to take her and only hearing from
afar the small still voice which was the voice of
sanity and preached sense to her:

A sudden ridiculous thought crossed her
mind. Was this Lesson Number Two? But then
Glenn pushed her away from him, as suddenly,
as abruptly, as harshly as he had pulled her
towards him. His voice grated through the daze
of her dreams. 'Don't teach me my business,
little Miss Gold-Digger, and do as you're told!'

Again the flat door slammed behind him and
the little ornaments on the side-table clinked.
His footsteps went down the corridor and
hushed into stillness. Aline rubbed her lips,
frantically, as if to rub away defilement, then

closed the fingers of both hands over them as if to treasure his touch.

Her emotions in a jumble, she decided she would go shopping, and buy what Glenn had said. There might be some reason in it. She would pay back every cent he lent her. She must drop her scruples and get on with the job in hand. There would be time enough to brood on that lonely station when the children were in bed. There would be time to think during her flight to Brisbane, however short it was. In the meantime she had to finish her packing. She must make a list of things, go to one of the big stores, where things might be less expensive, and choose and be glad that here shops stocked summer things while officially summer was a long time ahead. And she would have to ring Mrs Delamaine and thank her.

Which last she tried to do first. But there was no reply from Mrs Delamaine's number. Mrs Delamaine clearly was not at home.

Aline thought it would have been nice to have Jane or one of the other girls with her when she shopped. In London, of course, the intended purchase of each dress, pair of jeans or blouse had been discussed in great detail between the trainees and much advice, good or only well-meant, had been given. Generally several girls went along to give their opinion. But of course Jane and the others were working and might have plans for the evening, and, as it was not Thursday or Friday, the shops would not be open late anyhow. At least she did not think so. Aline caught the bus at the corner and went to the city.

The city offered huge stores, smart select boutiques and discount shops. She dawdled past half a dozen of these before she decided she was wasting time, so she went through one of the big revolving doors, her list of requirements clutched in a determined hand.

It was difficult to stay determined, however, when there were so many entrancing things that were not strictly essential and she had money in her purse. And the devil of temptation whispered. There was this dress, which was perhaps not really necessary, but then it would be useful if you might have to meet visitors. And there was that skirt and blouse with which you could play so many variations. And what about sandals—after all, there couldn't be snakes all over the place. Perhaps there weren't any at all. Surely where there were small children their father would see to it that no snakes would be tolerated. Perhaps it had just been Glenn's special sense of humour.

It was to the credit of Aline's sense and will-power that she kept to her list after all, or at least did until she was suddenly faced with a dress she simply could not resist. It was not the sort of thing you needed in the Outback. It was not the sort of thing a nursery nurse would need in the pursuance of her duties. It was not the sort of thing anybody *needed*, but it would be wonderful to have it. The price was not really all that high and it was really a sweetie.

Aline hesitated, finger on lips, moving from one foot to the other.

Behind her Mrs Delamaine spoke. 'How sensible of you to do some shopping! And that frock would suit you. Come on, try it on.'

'I don't really need it,' objected Aline, playing devil's advocate and wanting it more than ever. 'Oh, Mrs Delamaine, how are you? I was ringing you and ringing you and you weren't at home. I'm going to Brisbane tomorrow as nursery nurse to Mr Jennings' children—Mr Bill Jennings, that is.'

'What you need,' said Mrs Delamaine practically, 'is a cup of tea. Come along—that frock won't run away. And I bet you haven't had any lunch.' She bustled Aline into the lift and out into a bright, light and only half-filled restaurant. 'One can always talk here,' she explained grimly, 'because most people prefer the coffee lounge. And talk is what we need. Now just you tell me, child, what possesses you to bury yourself in the Outback? I've never heard such nonsense in my whole life! Gloria would certainly not approve of it. Of course, this is Glenn's idea, and what's behind it I'm sure I don't know, and I've known him for a good long time, but don't you give in.'

'I like working with children,' objected Aline, nibbling at a scone and finding it good. 'And the salary is excellent. I'll be able to save, and . . . ' But Mrs Delamaine did not let her get any further.

'No young person ever listens to her elders who have more sense, but from what I heard about you I thought you were a nice biddable girl, with some sense. How do you think you'll meet people in that back of beyond? How do you think you'll see a bit of Australia marooned at that station with no company but a couple of spoiled brats and a Jennings father who, being a Jennings, is impossible, though I'll admit less impossible than Glenn. How dear Gloria could have such a pair of grandsons I'm sure I don't know, and she the nicest person I've ever met. Aline, why don't you find yourself some nice job in a hospital or office or something?'

Mrs Delamaine sipped tea, Mrs Delamaine ate cakes, Mrs Delamaine crumbled scones and Mrs Delamaine talked, but what she did not do was listen. She apparently had never listened when Aline had explained that she needed and could not find a job. She apparently did not read the papers or listen to the radio, or pay attention to the television, at least as far as unemployment was concerned. The spate of words pouring from the exquisitely made-up lips gave the impression that employers all over the country were lining up, crying for the services of anyone graciously inclined to lend them a hand. But in the flood of words there was not the one sentence which would or might have persuaded Aline to change her mind—namely a reiteration of her invitation to stay with her indefinitely.

'Well, you young people don't listen, so you have to learn,' said Mrs Delamaine, gathering up parcels, handbag and—peculiarly enough—an umbrella. 'Come down and let's have a look at that frock. And do write to me.'

'I don't think I'll bother about the frock now,' said Aline, who had come to her senses now that the vision of lemon-yellow and snow-white was not in front of her.

'That stingy Jennings!' snapped Mrs Delamaine. 'I suppose you can't afford it. Come along, I'll buy it for you—and don't you dare to say a single solitary word!'

Aline said quite a few, but she might have saved herself the trouble. Mrs Delamaine did not listen, and all she said was that, as Gloria had been her closest friend, she felt it to be her right and duty—a very pleasant one—to buy the dress. And once the soft material was draped around Aline she stopped protesting. No girl in her senses could have done so.

'It's gorgeous!' she gasped. 'Oh, Mrs Delamaine, I've never had anything so beautiful. I ought not to let you, but thank you, thank you very much!'

There a peculiar smile on Mrs Delamaine's face. 'Don't worry, Aline. I'm getting as much fun as you out of it—more, if you but knew.'

'Oh,' said Aline blankly, and suddenly wished for no reason that she could understand that she had not accepted the gift. But it was obviously too late. And for some reason she found herself wondering what Glenn would think if he saw her in the dress.

The girls had arranged a surprise party for her that evening. They crowded into the room, approving her purchases. 'Very sensible,' said Jane. 'But oh, Aline, didn't you get anything really pretty? I wouldn't have been able to resist it. Where did you shop? But they do have really gorgeous things.'

Somehow Aline found she just could not bear to show them *the* dress and she did not know the reason. Surely there was nothing so very much wrong or even wrong at all in accepting a dress from an elderly lady in Mrs Delamaine's position, who wanted to give you some pleasure? But whatever her sense told her, she intuitively kept silent.

It was only when the others had gone and her flatmates, yawning, had sought their beds that her conscience overcame her. Jane had been so very good to her. Jane was not simply an acquaintance or a flatmate; she was a friend. So, sitting on her bed, watching Jane creaming her face, she said suddenly, 'Jane, there's one thing I didn't show you—I don't really know why. It's gorgeous and I shouldn't have accepted it, I know that, but . . . '

She flung open the wardrobe door to display emptiness, for all her things were packed, except the yellow dress with its heavy flounce. 'Here.'

'Aline, it's the tops! Why, it's just what you need. You'll look a treat in it.' Jane hesitated suddenly, remembering what Aline had said. 'Did you say—shouldn't have accepted it? Who—oh golly, don't tell me Glenn gave it to you! I wouldn't ever have believed it.' She stopped, staring, then said, 'I wouldn't have believed it of him. Not with a staff member. Aline, I shouldn't say anything and you can call me an interfering frog, but no, you shouldn't, not from Glenn.'

'Glenn?' asked Aline, so surprised that Jane drew a deep breath of relief. 'You don't think I would have taken it from Glenn? What do you think I am? You know I didn't even want to borrow money from him.'

'Sorry, love,' the other girl apologised. 'But if not Glenn—now don't hit the roof, of course I believe you, but if not Glenn, who? Give!'

'Mrs Delamaine,' said Aline, and put the dress carefully back on to its padded hanger. 'She saw me looking at it in the shop and she took me to tea and then insisted on buying it. And I wish I hadn't accepted it now, although I still don't know why. I just don't feel right about it, but it isn't that expensive, only Glenn will start his Miss Gold-Digger thing again if he finds out.'

'Not expensive?' echoed Jane, and turned the price ticket so that it glinted in the light. 'What do you call expensive?'

Aline looked and squeaked. 'Jane, I didn't notice! I thought fifty-three dollars, and while this is an awful lot for me . . . I misread.'

'By just a hundred dollars,' said Jane, and suddenly started to giggle. 'Well, it's done now, but if I were you I'd keep mum about it with Glenn. On the whole,' she added thoughtfully, 'I don't know that it wouldn't have been better to have accepted this from him, rather than from Mrs dear darling gossipy Delamaine, who's so sweet, I don't think.'

'I'll give it back,' said Aline, and fled for the cardboard box the dress had come in.

'You can't,' said Jane decisively. 'Not after having taken it. It's an insult. I wish you could, but you simply can't. Just forget about it.'

It was true. Aline knew she could not insult dear Mrs Delamaine, who was so old and disliked by many and yet meant so well. She carefully folded the dress into a suitcase.

CHAPTER FIVE

ALINE had liked very much what little she had
seen of Melbourne, the wide sweep of St Kilda
Road, with its mixture of beautiful old and
spartan new buildings; the broad boulevard of
Brighton Road, the narrow twisted alleys and
lovely roads of Toorak with their mansion-like
houses and their gorgeous blocks of flats; the
city with its conglomeration of plate-glass
emporiums and tiny luxurious boutiques; the
malls, and the busy roadways, the jingling
trams, panting buses, and the sleek or stocky
shapes of cars, limousines, snarling 'bombs'
and motorbikes. She had longed to explore the
Dandenong hills and mountains which were
hazing the horizon—to see little townships with
the peculiar and strange names of Olinda and
Sassafras, romantic and enchanting.

She had badly wanted to stare over blue val-
leys and take afternoon tea in small hostelries
which dreamed half-forgotten amidst the
gums, the wattles and the bushes. She had
eagerly awaited the blossoming of the wistaria

with its fairy blooms and had realised that Melbourne was beautiful.

But from the moment the jet had shaken off the grey net of enveloping cold cumulus clouds and dived through the atmosphere of flaming gold and silver, mother-of-pearl and scarlet, flashing reflected sunlight from each titanic wing, Aline fell in love with Brisbane. Yet if at that moment or later on somebody had asked her the reason for it, she could not have answered. Hazily, her mind too full of loveliness to function properly, she might have said that the kaleidoscope of colours, the warm breeze-laden scent of the sea, the tang of palms and scent of flowers, the gay clothes of the tourists, the shouting flute voices of the children off for a holiday, had made her feel so, but she would not have been able to say whether the houses were bathed in different tinges or the airport more beautiful than any she had seen or the people friendlier.

Even the realisation that nobody, absolutely nobody, had come to meet her could daunt her now. She thought, half resignedly, half humorously, that it was typically Jennings style and that it would be refreshing to meet one member of that clan who took after his grandmother instead of conforming to the Glenn pattern.

Then, having quartered the airport systematically in search of someone who was also searching for her, and having found nobody, she went over to the reception office and told the girl on duty who she was and that if anyone was looking for her she would be in the snack bar, and made her way there.

Through the big windows she could see the planes landing and taking off in a whirr of giant wings. She could see the blue sky patterned with white balls of cotton-wool. Her mouth tingled to the spicy tang of her tropical fruit drink, and she wondered what was in it. Mainly papaya, the friendly waitress told her, and reeled off a list of other ingredients, some familiar, some strange, but all enticing. Aline blinked her lashes into the yellow sunshine that flooded the room and wondered whether it was indeed she who was sitting here, in one of her new cotton frocks, happy and self-assured. Suddenly she heard herself addressed rather doubtfully. 'Miss Mellan? Is it Miss Mellan?'

By her side stood a bronzed young man with smiling lips and a rather puzzled look in his usually laughing eyes. She guessed his eyes were usually laughing because of the laughter-lines that radiated from them. He was as tall as Glenn, but there any resemblance between the brothers, if this indeed was Bill, stopped. Where Glenn was tight-lipped, arrogant and undoubtedly handsome, Bill was obviously relaxed, slightly stockier, dressed in a more off-the-cuff manner and determined to take life not too seriously. He said flatly, 'It can't be Miss Mellan.'

'I'm Aline Mellan,' said Aline with a smile, 'and I really don't see why I can't be me. Or is it I? I'm never sure over these finer points of grammar.'

'And who cares anyhow?' he agreed. 'I—me; well, we're both over school age and past the time for English grammar exams. Anyhow, some people say "I", and others "me", and who's to say who's right? I'm certainly not going to consult a grammar, even if I had one, and then I'd probably be unable to find the right page.'

Aline blinked her long lashes and, turning her head a fraction, saw herself pictured in a long mirror opposite, a girl in lime and white, with shining hair and shining eyes, and beside herself a young man whom not only she but any girl would like. A small bubble of laughter rose in her throat at this unusual conversation. She pulled herself together and did so with difficulty. She was not here to exchange light chitchat with a man, however romantic and pleasant. She was here to start her career as a nursery nurse.

'I'm certainly Aline Mellan,' she said, forcing her voice to primness. 'Are you—I mean, you are Mr William Jennings, the children's father?'

He sat down on another chair and waved at the waitress, ordering whatever was cold and ready, then turned back to her. 'But you can't be, girl. Glenn said you were middle-aged, and fully trained, but you're neither. I mean, you aren't middle-aged and you certainly aren't old enough to be trained. There's a muddle somewhere, and it makes a muddle of everything.'

Suddenly the sun was gone, although it was still painting arabesques on the floor. Suddenly the air was filled with mist, or seemed to be. Suddenly the job, the town, the lovely security of earning her living and being able to stay in this gorgeous place were gone too. Anxiously Aline explained. 'I'm only semi-trained, but I do assure you that I'm well able to cope with children. Two small ones don't worry me. I'm quite competent, and I do so love children.'

'Yes, I am Bill,' he said. 'And I couldn't care less whether you're trained or not. I just don't know why Glenn said that—but then Glenn never makes mistakes, or rarely, so I suppose I made the muddle. But it's a muddle all the same. Not your being able or unable to look after the twins—they're fairly good and I'm sure you could manage without any trouble. Anyhow, as long as you can keep them out of the dam or pull them out if they do fall in, which they seem to do all the time, I'm perfectly happy. If on top of that you can stop them from getting under my cousin's feet, I'd be more than obliged. No, the trouble is the cousin. She's still away on holiday, and although chaperons are out of fashion, the near-Outback—and country Queensland in particular—still don't like young and pretty girls staying in a bachelor's household, which, being divorced, I am to all intents and purposes. And how I'm going to get her back in a hurry I don't know. She housekeeps, I suppose Glenn told you, and she's keen on her holiday with her family. But there, not to worry. We'll manage somehow. Are you hungry? Well, if not, let's go and I'll book you into a motel and we'll see what we can do. There's no great hurry—the kids are with friends—and I can always find some business to do in Brisbane, so I can stay for a few days and you can sightsee, and I'll show you the surrounding countryside. No trouble whatever.'

'But—but are you sure it's convenient?' asked Aline.

He waved a large hand. 'I'll make it convenient, Nurse love,' he grinned. 'What's democracy for if we can't use our time as we like? And say—do I have to call you "Nurse"? I feel like something out of Jane Austen. Why not Aline? And I'm Bill. We don't stand on ceremony here in Queensland.'

Aline's mouth stayed open. Here was not only a man who behaved as no employer ought to behave, but also a member of the Jennings family who—whomever he took after—certainly was not made of the same material as his elder brother.

Aline found that whatever business Bill had in Brisbane certainly seemed ephemeral, for unless he did it before ten in the morning or after midnight, it simply was not done. These were the only hours she spent in her very smart motel unit, where she would have been quite happy to spend a lot more time, quite happy and even relieved, for she simply did not know how to cope with Bill, who apparently believed his duties as employer to his children's nurse extended beyond an employer-and-employee basis. He seemed always to want to be in Aline's company. And whenever Aline protested, saying, 'Mr Jennings, Bill I mean, I'm perfectly able to amuse myself,' he would laugh, shake his head and sweep her off to yet another restaurant, beach or children's furniture or toyshop to buy lavishly for his children, which, as he informed her outrageously, both disposed of his duties as a father and hers as the prospective nurse.

'I don't know whether I'm awake or asleep,' Aline told herself. 'I don't know how people like the Jennings live, but I can't believe there isn't a small hotel or pension or boarding house somewhere in Brisbane which wouldn't be more suitable to have put me into. This—this is gorgeous, but quite unreal.' She looked at the white-walled room, with its gay curtains, its divan bed, its tiny freezer and bigger refrigerator in the minute kitchen where there was not only an electric jug and saucepan and crockery, but also a cocktail shaker and a bottle of champagne. 'I'm here to start work, not for a— a honeymoon. This would make a good honeymoon suite.'

But when she asked Bill not to waste so much money unnecessarily, he merely opened his blue eyes and said that, as he was inconveniencing her by making stay in Brisbane for several days instead of settling comfortably in her new home, the least he could do was to make her comfortable.

'Of course, if you don't like it,' he said in mock-serious fashion, 'I can book you in somewhere else. Except that this is handy to the motel where I'm staying, so I hope you'll put up with it.

'Put up with it?' gasped Aline, thinking of the small room she had shared with a cousin, the sofa she had slept on at an elderly relation's, the bare clean accommodation in the orphanage, and the little better one at the nurses' hostel. 'This isn't my idea of "putting up" with it. This is luxury!'

'Now don't you be too easily satisfied,' grinned Bill, 'because I've found out that if you are, people take you at your word and then you don't get anything or anywhere. Just look at Glenn—he knows what he wants and he gets it.'

Aline thought it diplomatic to keep silent.

'You know what—we'll go to Surfers Paradise,' Bill said happily, 'I'd fly you over, but we have to land in Coolangatta and it's not worth it. I'll drive you. It's fun, that place, sort of the Miami of Australia, and you see all sorts of people there, elderly retirees and young would-be retirees and everyone in between, and the flowers are supposed to be wonderful. I've noticed you like flowers.'

'Are you sure your cousin isn't back yet?'

'What an idea!' grinned Bill. 'Though honestly I don't know. Look, let's see Surfers Paradise first and then I'll telephone. Promise so faithfully.'

The day was made for enjoyment, with the sea like a sheet of gold, the sun flaming in the molten sky and the gay white lacing of clouds scattered across it. Equally gay little houses flashed past, each in its square of garden, and restaurants which did not look like restaurants opened their patios and inside rooms to the tourists. 'Where the visitor is boss,' quoted Bill, 'and that's here all over the Gold Coast.'

'Gold Coast,' repeated Aline, savouring the word. 'Gold Coast.' Yes, that was what it was, a country full of golden beauty.

He turned off the highway before they reached the popular seaside city, whose skyscraper hotels towered into the sky, and moved along a heat-hazed avenue, where the palms and cacti mingled to create visual enchantment; large green monsters with long spikes, small narrow ones with flowers at their top, other in the most fantastic shapes, that even a science fiction author could not conceive. He stopped the car in front of a small house which seemed buried in the landscape. There were tiny tables beneath the trees and the sound of water from where a small brook sang between the stones.

'Beautiful!' gasped Aline, burying her small nose in the fruit drink which seemed native to Queensland.

'Man-made,' said Bill laconically. 'Tourist attraction—and helps the greenery. They grow their own vegetables and fruit—not that it's difficult here, as long as you have water. Aline, what do you want to eat?'

'Ice-cream, please,' said Aline, patting her hot face.

'Not ice-cream for starters. Definitely not. I'm all for the traditional in food.'

'I didn't think you were traditional in anything.'

'In food I'm a Tory of Tories. Hot or not, I want my meat, my spuds and my vegies. And my pudding too!'

However, what they got by Bill's choice was not traditional at all. There was what was called a 'seafood cocktail', tiny shrimps, minute crabs, floating pieces of lobster, delicious scraps of smoked salmon, oysters and a variety of other things buried in a spicy sauce. There was a mouthwatering rare steak, with attendant dishes of anything and everything, and finally Bombe Alaska—ice-cream, fruit and flaming cognac poured over the whole and lit.

'Ice-cream?' giggled Aline. 'Call that ice-cream? As much similarity to a simple cone as Van Gogh to a kindergarten daub!'

'It's frozen and certainly contains cream, ergo, it's ice-cream,' said Bill firmly. 'Aline, listen . . . '

The sky dreamed above them and the palms around. He was looking at her, not as Glenn had looked, not even as Jim had looked, but with hunger—and it was leaving her cold. As cold as the scraps on her plate, only that these were melting and her heart was not. Something in her mourned, because it would have been so right and fitting, so wonderful.

Aline picked up her white handbag and remembered when she had chosen it in London, in one of those tiny shops nestling in the shadow of emporiums, in a sale that offered what otherwise she could never have afforded. It had been for when she was going to be taken to meet Jim's parents, the event which had never happened. 'I'm dying to see Surfers Paradise,' she said, her voice uneven, and hoped Bill would not attribute its unevenness to himself, for that would be so bitterly unfair.

The streets of Surfers Paradise were jampacked with people shopping, people strolling around, people sampling the goodies in outside cafés. A busker attracted a languid crowd, and an ice-cream hawker had his white van surrounded by laughing, clamouring children. There were people sprawled on the yellow sands, their beach towels garish in vivid colours. 'Goodness, they can't move!' she laughed. 'It's like Blackpool on holiday!'

'Call that a crowd, love? It's off-season now, even if it's unseasonably hot. But June to August, December to February, that's when you really see this place jumping.'

'There can't be more people here than that without choking to death,' said Aline, doubtfully regarding the heaving, panting multitudes.

'Sez you,' said Bill, and deftly parked his car in a space for which a lot of others were jostling. 'Let's walk and see what gives.'

What Aline wanted to do more than anything was to have a ride in one of the glass-bottomed boats, and although she would never have asked, her eyes did it for her. 'Done it millions of times,' confided Bill, helping her in, 'but it's always nice.'

'Nice' wasn't what Aline would have called it. 'Entrancing' was what she would have used for the fairylike kaleidoscope of ever-changing shapes below her—something so breathtaking she knew she would never forget it. Branched corals like undersea trees, bushes and flowers, sea-monster-like etchings in shadow. Fish of all sizes were darting around. There was undersea vegetation which might be real or optical illusion but was the more enthralling for it.

'You ought to take up skin-diving, love,' Bill told her.

'Not me,' shuddered Aline. 'I'd die of fright!'

'We'll make a proper Aussie sheila of you yet!'

Aline refused to take the bait; she was much too busy staring around to listen to what anyone said.

'I adore these corals,' she breathed as she stood shakily on her legs again. 'Those colours—I never thought anything could be so beautiful. I'd just like to break off a piece and take it home to remember for ever.'

'They lose their colour when taken out of water without due care. At least, that's what they say.'

They searched for and found a shop specialising in corals and coral jewllery. Aline carefully chose a small medallion and asked for it to be wrapped, ready for transport to Aunt Helen. 'She'll love it. She adores pretty things and it will cheer her up when it rains. She's very old and very poor. And she was always good to me. She's really a great-aunt.' And she thought of Aunt Helen, living in one of those stereotyped little terrace houses, which was prim and proper from outside but had always the really-too-expensive bunch of flowers to brighten the sitting-room, and leaves in a vase and toy cacti in their pot.

'What about that?' asked Bill, holding up a rope of corals intertwined with gold and silver, fantastic in its loveliness. 'Wouldn't she like these?'

Aline gave a dim imitation of Jane's careless giggle as she thought of the small lady with her prim flannel gowns and sensible shoes. 'No, I think the medallion's much more suitable.' She did not say, 'and less expensive,' but again her face gave her away.

'Suits you,' said Bill, laconically throwing the rope across her shoulders, and yes, it did suit her. The colour flamed against the pale yellow and white of the very exclusive gown

Mrs Delamaine had given her, lit her face into animation and turned the sherry of her eyes into golden flame. She was suddenly beautiful.

'We'll have this,' said Bill to the saleswoman who had come up at the critical moment.

'Not for me,' said Aline, taking off the rope decidedly if rather reluctantly.

'Sure for you. A memento.'

But Aline dug her heels in and refused to take it.

The afternoon had melted into early evening and the shadows of night were painting the landscape. 'We'd better go,' said Aline, 'or we'll be very late. And you really ought to find out whether Mrs . . . Mrs . . . I mean your cousin is back. I'm dying to go on duty.'

They were sitting on one of the benches strategically placed as 'lookout', as they sleepily watched the moon painting its light over the clouds and the children being hustled off towards their evening meal, while the grown-ups strolled in the direction of restaurants or their apartment.

The sky was a tropical dream, not blue or grey or black, but a conglomeration of every colour of the rainbow, silver-hued, scarlet-tipped and ever-changing. Bill's arm lay on the back of the bench, very close to Aline's shoulders, but her thoughts were elsewhere and she did not notice. From across the waters, where a pleasure launch was moored, a stream of continental music caressed the waves and the air streams.

'Aline,' said Bill.

'Mmm . . . '

'Aline . . . ' and she was in his arms. It should have been ecstatic, but it was not. She was utterly unable to respond. She felt him draw back.

'Aline,' he said again, and she turned to him, eyes deep-shadowed, mouth lifted.

'Oh, damn it,' he muttered, and jumped to his feet. 'Oh, damn it, Aline!'

Over the romantic dreaming sand with the dampness of the surfing breakers they walked to where the car was parked. 'I'm sorry,' said Aline finally in a small voice.

'You're a baby,' he said, not roughly, not gruffly, but with hurt in his voice, and revved up and directed the snarling monster through the towns and villages which were still bright with sightseers, past the tourists and the locals, some of them aboriginals, who seemed no different in dress and style from the whites.

'They're assimilated here, at least outwardly,' Bill explained, and she sensed that he was glad to have a harmless topic of conversation. 'Once at home you'll meet the real thing, and I know you'll like them. They're nice—and interesting.'

The next morning, Bill having presumably spoken to his cousin, they finally set out for the station.

Having flown for so many thousands of miles should have weaned Aline of airsickness and flying fear, but she found it was one thing to travel in a jet scything through the air, and another to sit in a small single-engined plane, piloted not by experienced and reliable pilots, but by a young man who was emotionally upset. The sky seemed to descend and slap her face; the ground seemed to rush up and bump her feet. She thought ruefully that if going by air was the only way from Bill's property it would take a great deal to make her decide to leave.

'Soon be there,' said Bill, in a sudden change of mood, obviously enjoying himself. 'Like it?'

'No,' Aline said firmly. 'I'm going to be airsick any moment if you don't stop this—this jiggling.'

'Oh glory, I forgot! You've never been in a small plane before.'

'Certainly not in one piloted like this,' was what Aline wanted to say, but, her heart in her mouth, she could only nod agreement.

Finally the earth rushed up, the clouds raced past, the trees passed by and she suddenly saw the narrow strip of tarmac. Bill raced the plane through the atmosphere, straightened it and took it in a flat spin, and Aline, holding on with all her strength, gasped, 'Why, this is incredible!'

Incredible it was—the wide plains, the grazing cattle, the sprawling homestead and the people who were coming from all directions to cluster round the small building at the end of the runway. There were men in pants and boots, others in shorts but with equally heavy footwear; there were some women, their cheeks brown with the sun and their eyes wide with laughter, who waved to the incoming and circling plane. And there were children—with faces like velvet, brown bare toes scuffing the ground, small bunched fists also waving freely.

'They're the most glorious kids I've ever seen,' gulped Aline. 'Tell me, Bill, can our children play with them? Do say they can!' For Aline had lived in Melbourne long enough to realise that some people here, as elsewhere, and strange as it might seem, just kindly condescended to the original settlers of the land.

'Just you try to keep them apart!' he grinned, taking one hand off the joystick in order to wave back. 'Why, they've been friends since they could crawl. Just make sure they don't get into the dam.' It was a reiterated echo of all he had said before. 'And—thanks for saying "ours".'

Blood flushed into Aline's cheeks, for how could she explain to this man that all chidren's nurses, nannies, nursery nurses, children's wards, highly-qualified Sisters and the like called their charges 'our' children, without any interest in their parents, male or female. She said, 'Where are they, then?' her voice softer than it had been since last night.

Bill waved towards the end of the strip, 'Over there, holding hands. They always cling, I suppose because of being twins. Oh, no, Aline! Just look!' Suddenly the laughter was wiped off his face. 'Don't tell me that that blasted brat has run away from school again. I don't know what we'll do with her. The Head said last time that she'd not take her back. Really, it's too much!'

Behind the throng of people who—as Bill had explained earlier on—worked on the property or on government projects, stood a girl of about ten or eleven, a pale child with a determined mouth and lips that were pressed harshly together. She wore the sort of expression which any experienced children's nurse would have equated with trouble. Yet something about the blank eyes, the taut stance of the shoulders, woke Aline's pity. 'She must have been very unhappy there,' she remarked.

'She'll be much unhappier when I get to her,' said Bill icily. 'I've just about had her and her tantrums!'

The plane's undercarriage bumped, the wheels gripped and they went past the throng in a rush of air and taxied to a standstill. Aline felt herself brushed aside as the tots hurled themselves into their father's arms.

'Oh, isn't it hot?' she gasped, trying to blink the sun out of her eyes.

'It will be hotter still,' snapped Bill, for a moment looking exactly like his brother and sounding like him too, but Aline knew his temper was not directed against her, but rather against the tall, rather gangling child, Jill, who was coming forward sullenly, already expressing her feelings. 'I'm not going back, I'm not! I'm not!'

They were inside the homestead, where the air-conditioning whirred and there was ice-cold tea with lemon. The almost frozen droplets ran gratefully down Aline's parched throat and the tots, wide-eyed, were looking at her and soon responding to her smiles. She smiled at Jill too, but got only a cold stare as her answer.

'And if you're not going back,' snapped Jill's father, 'or if Miss Forbes won't take you back, for which I wouldn't blame her for a moment, where will you get your education? Or do you consider it's finished at eleven? And even if you can convince me of that, and I'm so tired of your tantrums that I'd be willing to accept almost anything, how are you going to convince the Education Department of it? Don't you know you haven't reached school-leaving age?'

'I'm not going back.' Jill's voice was flat, toneless and desperate.

'After having run away from two schools do you really think another will accept you? Because if you do, I don't. Also I'm not willing to outfit you with new uniforms, take you to a new place and then run into the same type of trouble as before. You can just sit down here and write to Miss Forbes with an apology, and I hope for your sake that she's willing to accept it.'

Jill burst into tears. 'I'm not going back! I want to go to a day school. I hate boarding schools, I want to live in a normal home.'

'And where,' demanded her father, 'am I going to find a day school for you? You know as well as I do that there's none around here.'

Uncomfortably, Aline felt he was being too hard on the child.

'I don't want to stay here. I haven't got any friends here. I can't go to a theatre or to the movies or to any places where other girls my age go. I want to live in Melbourne. And Mrs Delamaine would take me, you know she would. She'd be thrilled to take me—she said so.'

'You are not going to stay with Mrs Delamaine.' Bill's voice was so much like Glenn's that Aline involuntarily glanced around to see whether he was in the room. 'Like any other child in the Outback you're going to get your schooling at a boarding school and spend your holidays in your own home. Anyhow, it's all my own fault. If I didn't give in to you all the time and believe your promises, I would have given your allowance to your housemistress and you wouldn't have been able to run away.'

Jill refused to pick up that gauntlet. 'All Outback children don't go to boarding school. There's such a thing as correspondence lessons, and I can't see why I can't have them. Others do. Lots do.'

'Seeing that I can fortunately afford to send you to a first-class school where you can enjoy all the things you claim you want to do, you are not going to have correspondence lessons. Any other girl would be more than grateful. And this time I'm not standing for any nonsense. I'm going to get in touch with Miss Forbes, and back you go—that is, if she'll have you.'

Jill stuttered, 'I—I'll run away again. I'll keep on running away. If I don't have any money I—I'll hitch-hike and I'll get here somehow. So there!'

'What are these correspondence lessons?' asked Aline.

Bill wheeled around on her and suddenly sported the old grin. 'The brat's going to go back, but I doubt whether Miss Forbes is going to have her straight away, and in the meantime, you can teach her. It's as easy as winking, and by the end of the term she'll realise, I hope, that it's as boring as can be here for her and that she ought to have some sense. And don't tell me, Jill, that you're going to Mrs Delamaine. Mrs Delamaine is a mischief-making old . . . Oh well, a very nice old lady who doesn't realise how much of a minx you are and who certainly doesn't have the strength to cope with you. And what's more, there's no reason why she should. We aren't related. So say how do you do to your new governess, and for goodness' sake, behave. You've spoilt everything, as you usually do. I don't know what I've done to deserve a brat like you!'

Aline gasped. Jill glared at her with dislike, mumbled something and rushed out of the room.

Bill shrugged his shoulders in exasperation. 'If I'm born again, I'll become a monk,' he sighed. 'In an enclosed order where they don't teach and nobody under eighteen's ever admitted. Sorry to have let you in for this, Aline. My cousin's going to be back tonight. Your room is just at the end of that corridor.' He stood up and turned to the twins who, hand in hand, faced him, the corners of their lips turned down and tears threatening. 'I've brought you lots of toys and Aline will play with you. Say hello to her nicely and show her to her room.'

Aline felt her hands grasped by two soft little ones. 'Me show you,' said the fair-haired twin, and beamed.

'Me show you too,' said her echo. 'And Auntie Belle be here soon.'

The room had polished floors, gay short curtains, heavy blinds to exclude the sunlight

and first-class air-conditioning. One door led
to Aline's own bathroom. There were also soft
deep armchairs and a small cane table. There
was a cane-headed bed, some bookshelves
crammed with books, and scatter rugs on the
floor.

Some hours later the housekeeping cousin
arrived, a tall svelte woman, perfectly and
plainly dressed, and just as surprised at Aline's
youthfulness as Bill had been.

'I do hope you'll be very happy here, Miss
Mellan. We're a very quiet household, but of
course any time you want to get into the nearest township just let me know and I'll see what
I can arrange. I do hope you'll settle in quickly.'
Her smile was pleasant, her voice was pleasant,
and yet in the most agreeable way she soon
managed to tell Aline that no governess or
nurse had ever stayed long at the station.

'Well, you can't blame them for it, poor
things. Glenn and Bill are quite mad about the
place and they simply won't understand that
any woman wants something more than a
place, however lovely that is, at the back of
beyond, with children who've been allowed to
run wild and play with every other mannerless
child on the place, and where we don't even
have television. Well, it's been promised by the

government again and again, and no doubt we'll get it here sooner or later, but for the time being all we have is horse-riding—you do ride, don't you?—and the gramophone and the wireless, although the reception isn't at all marvellous, and what with the dam you can't even take your eyes off the kids, and the snakes make walks a problem. Well, as I said, I hope you'll be very happy, and it will be a great relief to me if you are.'

CHAPTER SIX

ALINE plunged into her work, ran and played
and cuddled the twins and got on with them
from the first moment; ploughed on deter-
minedly with her lessons with Jill and had the
gratification to win at least some of the girl's
confidence, so that Jill told her she had hated
her school, hated the staff and hated the other
girls. 'A mouldy horrid lot, with not a gram of
sense between the lot of them,' and that Aline
was not bad for an oldie. She managed to keep
a straight face at the backhanded compliment
and pleased Jill by playing tennis with her by
the hour.

She found to her surprise that she was not
expected to do any of the chores any children's
nurse expects to do, such as washing the tots'
clothes and looking after the nursery as far as
superficial cleaning was concerned. The velvet-
cheeked, velvet-eyed aboriginal girls with their
perfect courtesy, who comprised the domestic
staff, with giggles and shakings of head, pulled
out of her hands any item she wanted to clean,

brush, polish, iron or do anything whatever with, and even her personal undies were done. Flashing-eyed, the aboriginal matrons approved of her handling of her charges and looked on smilingly while she played with every child on the place. The sun shone, the breeze was soft from the south—which Aline found, in Australia, meant cool—and everyone agreed that they had not had such a nice spring for ages. Even the weather forecasters were optimistic.

And best of all, she thought, there was still no sign of Glenn. She was beginning to have fun; now that she had stopped feeling quite so much 'the new chum', and there were whole days when Jim had been consigned into the limbo of the gladly forgotten and she hardly remembered his face or his lips or the lure of his voice. She decided she was going to have a good time.

When she got her first month's salary she penned a stiff little note to Glenn, enclosing a cheque in part-payment, and felt a special sense of satisfaction. Once she had paid off what she owed the Jennings, she thought, everything would be plain sailing.

One morning when the jackaroo came back with the mail she had a letter from Mrs Delamaine. The heavy beautiful paper with its engraved initials was like something from another age. But then Mrs Delamaine belonged to a different generation, brought up in a more leisurely and formal fashion. Except that there was nothing very leisurely or formal about Mrs Delamaine's letter, if you could call it a letter, and not a command. For Mrs Delamaine, in half a dozen imperious straight lines, told Aline it was utterly unsuitable for her to stay at the station, 'being a servant to your godmother's grandson and maid to his children,' and ordered her to return to Melbourne where she would find her a suitable job with one of her friends, who all would like a 'well-bred young woman as companion-help'. And she was expecting her at the end of the week, 'as I suppose you will have to give some days' notice.'

'Well, of all the cheek!' exclaimed Aline, rattled from her habitual good temper. 'What does she think I am?'

'A very nice person,' said Jill, to her surprise, Aline having temporarily forgotten the presence of her generally troublesome charge. 'Whoever has written it. And if you don't like it, tear it up and forget it.'

Aline agreed that it was a very nice letter and she had been thinking of something else entirely, and whisked herself out of the room.

This extremely nice and beautiful country, with its pleasant and kindly people, who went out of their way to make her welcome, seemed unfortunately also to contain some who went beyond the bounds of sensitivity. For it was none of Mrs Delamaine's business where she worked, nor was it Mrs Delamaine's business to interfere, and if she already thought that having been friend to Aunt Gloria entitled her to it, why had she not objected more strenuously when first being told, or offered her a different job at that time? And what was there to object to? If it was a moral situation to which Mrs Delamaine objected, her objections were groundless, because Belle was there as a chaperon.

'She must be off her rocker,' said Aline, unaware that she was not alone.

'I don't know who you're referring to, but I agree with you. On principle,' said Bill.

She felt his arm around her and his mouth on her own. She drew herself aside and laughed. 'Oh, do give over, Bill!' she scolded, finding that goodnatured banter worked best in holding Bill at arm's length. 'And it's Mrs Delamaine. I know she's sweet; I know she means well. I know she was a friend of Aunt

Gloria's, but why, oh, why does it matter to her that I work for you?'

'Mrs Delamaine's the most accomplished actress I know. She missed her vocation. She's also the opposite of kind, the opposite of sweet, and if she was a friend of my grandmother's except in her own mind I never ever heard about it. Oh, she was an acquaintance of Gloria's. They sat on some welfare boards together and I believe they went to the same school in the dear old days, but Gran was nobody's fool, and you can believe me. You give me that letter and I'll deal with dear darling, not-at-all-beloved Mrs Delamaine.'

'Please, no,' urged Aline, hiding the letter behind her back. 'I shouldn't have told you. Bill, let be. Let be, Bill, please!'

'Oh, okay,' shrugged Bill. 'No use wasting any time on that besom—which for your translation is an old-fashioned word for witch.'

'I also read classics, and on top of it I dote on Regency romances and I know more old-fashioned words than you. Bet you,' said Aline crushingly, and whisked herself on to the grass and set off in furious pursuit of four twinkling legs as the twins made for their favourite and most forbidden place. 'I'll murder those kids of yours one day!' she threw over her shoulder.

The days passed. The heat rose and rose and the grass was parched yellow. The level of the dam fell almost daily and Bill went around muttering dark threats to all wildlife predators, including birds. 'I need my water,' he told Aline, when she rose in their defence. 'My cows are thirsty.'

'Don't you think all those others—kangaroos and birds or whatever—are also thirsty? I think that fence is cruel, and I'm glad that the birds at least have wings.' There were high spots of colour in Aline's cheeks and she put her hands across them. 'Thirst hurts.'

'And don't you think, my little English country Miss, who doesn't know what drought means, that cows and other domestic animals feel thirst just as much as does wildlife? Have you ever seen what a—a cow looks like when you have to shoot it because it's past saving? And those cows are my responsibility.' She had not heard Bill sounding so cross before.

'I think it's simply hateful—all that heat, all that drought, all that . . . that miserable . . . ' Aline bit her lip and ran into the house.

'Hey, wait! Here are some letters for you,' called Bill, returning to his calm self. 'And—

pax, Aline. This isn't your fault and it's not mine, either.'

She gave him the ghost of her usual smile, and looked at her mail. Time passed so quickly here that she had not even been able to reply to Mrs Delamaine, although what kept her so busy she did not know. She had written to some of her friends in England—'How we coped with dozens of babies and yet managed to have regular time off I'm sure I don't understand any more. These two little minxes here keep me busy from morning to evening, and Jill adds her quota. If I only could arrange to work to a time-table this wouldn't happen. It may be the enervating heat, or that hospital methods don't work in a private home.'

However, hot or not, she would have to answer Mrs Delamaine this evening, but she wondered how she was going to refuse her royal command without hurting the old lady's feelings.

She turned over to her envelopes. There was one from England; the other was from Melbourne. Her heart leapt and missed a beat. Who could write to her from Melbourne but Mrs Delamine and the girls at the flat, and none of these would type their letters. Or—or it could be Glenn? Of course, that was it. He had received her cheque and told his secretary to acknowledge it.

Aline felt a curious sense of anticipation as she touched the paper which he might have handled. She inserted the small paperknife from her bureau and the note tumbled out, with her cheque heavily scored through.

Dear Miss Mellan,' wrote Glenn (or his secretary), *'I am returning your cheque as you owe me nothing and should have the sense to know it. My grandmother brought you out, and whether I approve of that or not I do feel responsible for you.*

'Under these circumstances and seeing that I sent you into Queensland, it's up to me to supply you with the proper outfits for that very taxing climate. Please don't write to argue. I've wasted more than enough time on you and your affairs, as you refuse to co-operate. I hope this is the last time I have to concern myself with your antics.'

Aline looked out of the window, at the big moon swimming in its bath of cumulus, at the night birds screaming across the barren land-scape, at the faint nimbus of the hot and panting earth. 'Now I've heard everything—or read it, rather,' she considered. Not the rude-ness. Glenn not being rude would mean that there was something seriously wrong with him. But his feeling responsible . . . Oh, blow the man! And, to her surprise, two hot tears ran down her hot face.

The hot breeze wafted through the fly-wire screens. Some stars shone on the horizon. Through the half-open window she saw the station cat stalking some prey. The land was beautiful and almost frightening, in a way that made her crouch lower and peer into the darkness. And she might have stayed like that for a second, a minute or for hours or dropped off into a nightmare, or listened half-awake to the night sounds. But suddenly she was wide awake and upright.

Her eyes were wet with tears, for she knew not what reason, and she sought for a hand-kerchief and finally found one. She pressed her nose against the fly-wire mesh and told herself that the cry of a night bird must have startled her—or perhaps the moan of a thirst-ridden cow or steer, or some bovine mother bawling for her calf.

'I'll get myself a glass of water,' she told herself, and pushed her hair off her forehead, the heavy hair which seemed so limp in the heat, for darkness or not, the heat brooded over the house and the paddocks and bare patches around, and even the air-conditioning inside seemed powerless. Aline again blinked her lashes, then saw two little figures, hand in hand as usual, running swiftly, running noiselessly, towards the forbidden dam, at an hour when they ought to have been snug in their cots.

The sporadic moonshine drew glints of shiny red from one little head, yellow beams from the other. She struggled with the window catch, leaned out and called, 'Come back here! Twins, come back instantly!' and launched herself through the aperture in hot pursuit.

Before her, shapes danced on the barren ground and what few flowers had survived rustled in the dry wind. Some of the station dogs set up a frantic barking. Behind her she saw lights going on and, coming suddenly to her senses, she paused for one second to yell, 'Bill, Mrs Jackson—the children are at the dam!' then caught her breath and leaned against the breeze, aware of the swoop of some night thing, of the impediments of stones and sparse growth beneath her feet. She screamed again and knew that the wind blew the words out of her mouth and hurled them into the wastes, and also that she would not make it, not in time, and she became frantic. Her breath sobbed in her lungs and throat, her heart was banging like a wild thing and her chest laboured. 'Twins, back here!' She blinked her eyes and looked again at the dam which was etched against the sky and at the two little figures jumping up and down at the edge. 'Come back here at once, do you hear me?'

The twins were quite good usually about coming when called, but never had they tried to get out at night, whatever mischief they got up to during the day. Never. Not only in the short time that she had been here, but even before. Bill had said so. Mrs Jackson, who certainly was always more than willing to criticise the children, had said so. Even Jill had said so. 'I used to, you know, Aline, but they don't. I don't know why, but they honestly don't.'

What on earth had made them come out now, so late, Aline wondered, into the hot night of impending storm? And why didn't they at least turn back and grin at her, as they did during the day, when caught trying to do what they now looked like succeeding at?

'Libby, Nan—come back here at once!' Her voice was high in her own ears, but she knew they would not hear it, capering there, shaken with laughter and mirrored by the heaving waters which were being played with by the wind. The dam was low now, but not low enough to be safe for such small children. And if they jumped, if they fell, they could easily hit their heads on stones or other rubbish. She put on a last spurt of strength and with heart-stopping horror saw that one of them had disappeared while the other twin just stood there blankly and then ran.

Where, oh, where was the children's father? Where was Belle Jackson? Where were the jackaroos? Wasn't anyone trying to save them? Wasn't anyone there? Hadn't anyone heard her? Her legs were trembling. She fell heavily over a stone she had not seen and, striving shakenly to get up, heard behind her what seemed the sound of laughter.

She could not spare the time to turn and investigate. She had to do it all on her own. No, somebody was coming up behind her. But the thought that one of those shining-haired tots was drowning, pulled down by her own weight into those heavy depths, was too much. She must not stop.

Now she was at the rim of the dam. She pulled at the cord of her fortunately short dressing-gown, could not undo it, and, ignoring the shouting which had just risen behind her, went in, floundering towards a dark shape which moved sluggishly beneath the surface.

She swallowed water and was sick. She could not see, but she tried to blink the water out of her eyes. She could not move, but somehow she was moving. She struck out desperately with stinging eyes and labouring breath and the pain in her chest getting worse and worse. How big was that dam? How long would it take her to locate that child?

Something loomed up before her—a floating log. She did not see it until it was too late, and crashed full into it. The force of the smash caught her high up on the temple. Sickness and vertigo blotted out the stars. Cold water brought them back, them and the noise and— yes, incredibly, still the laughter.

'Listen, you fool girl!' That was Bill, by her side, holding her. 'Stop! Stop!'

But how could she stop? How could he? Libby or Nan was in, perhaps drowning. She fought him savagely, pulled loose and sank. He caught her again and held her, with her hands behind her back. He had her at the edge of the dam and had almost got her on to dry land. And finally her vocal chords did their job. 'You fool!' came the hoarse whisper. 'Libby or Nan, in there. Too late. Try . . . ' She tried herself to get back into the dam and fell to her knees.

'Aline—Aline, stop it! Libby and Nan aren't in there. They were trying to fool you and they ducked. They frightened the wits out of Belle once like that and they've since tried it on anybody and everybody, but never with the success of tonight. Aline, I'm sorry, I ought to have told you. I don't know what made me forget, but it hasn't happened for some time.'

The water ran down her shortie dressing-gown, over the almost transparent nightie. Her hair was limp, in rats-tails around her tear-bloated face. She blinked her eyes again—for the millionth time this night, or so it seemed to her—then she saw them standing there, safe and well and secure, two little shapes with laughter-widened months and their solid little bodies shaking with little giggles. Behind them she saw the jackaroos and the other men of the station staff, most of them laughing at her because she did not know when she was being fooled.

With the sudden relaxation of fear, the sudden relief, Aline felt furious. She looked around her, at poker-faced Belle Jackson who had told her that no governess lasted long here. At Jill who, to her credit, tried hard not to laugh but could not quite make it. At Bill, now concerned, but with the laughter-creases still around his eyes and lips.

And Aline did what every nursing Sister and child-care lecturer strictly forbade. She picked up the giggling children, one after the other, and applied a good old-fashioned slap on their wriggling rears.

'There!' she said furiously. 'Maybe this will teach you to do as you're told!'

She stared around her into the stunned silence and added defiantly, looking straight at Bill, 'And I'm going to save you the trouble of sacking me: I'm sacking myself. I'll leave first thing in the morning, even if I have to walk to the nearest public transport to get myself out of here. And you can keep your reference. Not that you owe me one after this!'

'Aline——' Bill began.

'That girl needs some good hot coffee,' said Belle Jackson.

'I'll take you if you really want to go,' said a good-looking jackaroo defiantly. 'And if anyone objects, I'll leave too.'

'The whole lot of you are crazy!' protested Bill. 'Aline, listen . . . '

But Aline had had more than enough. She brushed past them, stumbled, recovered herself and with a strength she had not known she still possessed ran back to the house and made a dive for her bathroom and pushed the bolt to.

The door rattled. 'Aline, it's me, Bill. Open up at once!'

Aline wanted to tell him exactly what he could do with himself but contented herself with a simple, 'No!'

'Please, please, Aline, come out! You'll be sick.' Jill was crying.

'Miss Mellan, if you stay in there you could be very ill indeed. You've had a nasty shock and you're soaking wet.' Belle was concerned and practical.

'Don't worry, I won't be here to be a burden on you if I am. There are hospitals, and good ones. And if I had had any sense I would have waited for a hospital job instead of coming to this madhouse. Just go away and leave me. Because I'm not coming out until you're all gone—all of you! And I'd like to change into something dry.'

Then there was silence, blessed silence.

Aline clapped her hands to her forehead, which was suddenly boiling hot, while the rest of her froze. If she did not get off that floor she would be ill and the Jennings would have to nurse her, which was something she certainly did not want. She ought to get into bed. There were extra blankets in the nursery and she ought to get there and take them.

She tried to stand, holding on to the low bath and then to the basin. Memory came back in slow hazed waves. The twins. The dam. Oh yes, the twins had fooled her and she had smacked them and Bill had sacked her. No, she had sacked herself.

'Let me in, Aline!'

Aline shakily got to her feet, just as the door crashed and sent her flying. The little bolt had been of no use; it had not held. With a sudden flash of memory, she remembered she had said something like that before, or thought it. Only then it had been 'would be of no use'. And it had not been hers. It had been in the flat in Melbourne, and she had not tried to evade Bill, But Glenn. And with a sudden, blinding flash she was thinking how wonderful it would be to be taken care of by a man like Glenn.

CHAPTER SEVEN

THE HEAT was increasing and the air-conditioning was fighting a losing battle. Outside a humid breeze beat against the windows, carrying hot sand. It would be lovely to be in the middle of winter. Aline closed aching eyes in an aching head and wondered if she would ever be cool again—or ever have a head that did not ache or eyes that did not ache, or a heart—there was no doubt about it—that did not want, of all people, Glenn. Glenn of the stony heart and the stony eyes and the heartbreakingly warm smile, for other people and not for her.

She pressed her lips together tight. Had it been her fault that he had always treated her with so much—so much contumely? Had she not taken offence so easily, smiled at him instead of frowning, things might have been different.

No, they wouldn't. They couldn't. This bang on the head must have sent her batty.

The door opened and Belle came in, the tray in her hands loaded with dishes and a lovely smell of egg and bacon preceding her. 'There,' she said, would-be cheerful. 'I do hope you're feeling better. Nothing like a good breakfast to help one! She carefully poured out a cup of coffee, adjusted the glass dish with fruit salad, in which papayas and pineapples predominated. 'I do hope you'll like these. The croissants are just out of the oven.'

Aline neither looked at her nor said anything.

'You will try and eat something, won't you?' said Belle, puzzled and quite obviously worried.

Aline looked through her, which needed a shift of her eyes of about two inches. 'No.'

'You must. You'll get very weak.'

Aline shrugged, feeling in fact too weak to argue.

Some hours later Bill came in. He stood in the doorway, looking anxious. 'Aline, Belle is worried to hell. If you're feeling worse we can get the doctor back. But you know he advised bed rest only.' Despite the fact that the blinds were drawn he squinted as if against strong sunlight.

Aline persisted. 'No,' she said simply.

'Aline, listen to me. I know you're feeling awful. You've had a shock and a bang on the head. If you're really crook, I'll fly you to the nearest hospital. Would you like that?'

She looked at him quickly, memories of her last flight with Bill still in her mind. She shook her head and Bill, looking defeated, turned and left the room.

Then Jill came, appearing through the window, her voice subdued. 'I'm sorry, I should have warned you, but I didn't think. Those awful brats—I could murder them! Are you very ill? I'm really sorry, and you do look awful.' Her voice wobbled.

At this, Aline suddenly found herself sitting bolt upright in her bed and looking with critical solemnity at her image in the mirror opposite. 'I do, don't I?' she said simply. 'And I feel worse. And I'm going to get up and get packed and get out of here—now! She swung her feet out of bed, tried to stand and collapsed back, but docilely drank the iced lemonade Jill held to her lips.

Bill soon appeared again. 'Well, I'm glad you've been able to stop saying, 'No', Aline,' he said. 'And I'm sorry about it all. I know what concussion does to you—I've had it a couple of times. But it usually wears off quickly.'

'I'll try to get back to the children tomorrow,' promised Aline stiffly. 'I have every intention of working out my notice.'

'Who's given you your notice?' Bill reacted sharply. 'I didn't, and I employ you.'

'I'm leaving, all the same.' she said. 'There's not the least doubt about that. And don't blame the twins, they were simply the last straw that broke the camel's back—my back. I'll get back to Melbourne or Brisbane and I'll try to work my way back to England, and I'll continue my nursery training or go as a char or go on the dole—but I'm not staying anywhere where there are Jennings!'

'There must be a lot of Jennings in England,' objected Jill, appearing in the doorframe. 'And I can't help being a Jennings, even though I don't want to be. And I want you to stay. Who's going to teach me if you leave? I didn't jump or pretend to jump into the dam, and I won't be punished for what I didn't do, and I won't go back to school. So you've got to stop. Do you hear me, Aline, you've got to stop! Anyone's better than school, and as for the Head there . . . '

Aline suddenly felt like laughing, but Bill was serious.

'What's wrong with the Jennings?' he demanded indignantly. 'I'd have thought we're a pretty nice bunch. I know Glenn sometimes comes the high and mighty, but he doesn't really mean it.'

'Anyhow, I can't look after the twins,' said Belle, dumping another tray. 'You stay in bed, and get really well, and don't you stand any nonsense from anyone. Jobs aren't all that easy to get anyhow, and you could do worse than us.'

Aline stared wordlessly at the ceiling, and finally the night came. The night and reflections and the knowledge that although all that Jill and Bill and Belle had said was true, the real reason why she was going to stay was that if she did not, she would lose her last link with Glenn. She thumped her wet pillow and went to sleep.

After nearly a week, she got shakily back to her feet.

'Me sorry,' said Nan, throwing her arms around Aline when she tottered into the lounge.

'Me sorry too,' said Libby, screwing up her baby mouth, and even meaning it for the moment.

Not believing it for an instant, having had experience of children and their short memories for ill-deeds, Aline yet hugged them. A warm bundle of child in her arms gave her a feeling of comfort.

But really there was little time for brooding, for wondering whether she had been foolish or wise in tacitly agreeing to stay, because things started to hot up, not only weather-wise, but also in the tempo of preparations as the party drew nearer. Jill went peacocking around in her new party frock and Belle's visits to the nearest township became more frequent, as she went for her fittings to the French dressmaker, who had migrated to Australia some years back and who had found a most appreciative clientele among the wives and daughters of the various property owners, as well as among the professional women around.

'Plain cream with black edgings,' said Belle, describing her frock in detail. 'Pure silk, which is always nice.'

'Oh, of course, lovely,' agreed Aline, who had never been nearer to pure silk than admiring it when window-shopping. 'Really beautiful!' She nearly added, 'It must be expensive,' but suppressed it at the last moment. And really, there was nothing to be surprised about. Although officially Belle was Bill's housekeeper, Aline had realised long ago that she must have a very solid income of her own. Why, then, did Belle work as Bill's housekeeper, Aline had often wondered. After all, if it was merely the urge to work, Belle could have found something more interesting to do. It was not as if she was an outdoor person, who enjoyed sport, or was especially fond of children

'I really don't know what to do,' Aline confided to Belle one day, just after breakfast. 'I've got a very nice party frock, but it's much too dressy for a picnic. For the rest, there isn't anything halfway suitable. I wonder whether I ought to make myself a nice pants-suit.'

'Why don't you come with me next time I go into town?' asked Belle. 'There are a number of good shops, and you might just find something you like. Let's go tomorrow. And *no*, we are *not* taking the twins! The cook can look after them, or Bill can drown them, or the dogs can sit guard on them, but I want a few hours of peace and quiet, and if you don't, you ought to.' She smiled, but obviously meant it.

The township was one of those typically Australian ones which you see all over the continent—a wide high street, with shops on both sides, some discount stores for those who had to count cents, and boutiques for those who could let their taste rule their head, and where the sky was the limit. A few milk bars and a lot of chemists' shops which sold everything from cosmetics to toys to scuffs and even medicines. There were coffee lounges and there was a park which was being watered out of a bore and therefore green and inviting. There were ice-cream parlours and take-away shops and restaurants. There were residential streets intersecting the main road, lined with weatherboard and brick veneer houses and the occasional solid brick. Wide verandas shielded the windows from the glare of the sun and some palm trees shook their fronds. And there was sunshine, blaring, glaring, biting sunshine which defied the protection of sunglasses.

'The bazaar,' said Jill, once Belle had vanished into a smart and soignée boutique which would have suited Nice or Monte Carlo or Juan-les-Pins. 'They've got some gorgeous materials. I do wish I could sew.'

'Didn't you have needlecraft lessons at school?' asked Aline, still wondering whether she was not being extravagant and ought to wear Mrs Delamaine's lovely gift. Somehow she felt it was just not the thing—not because it was too party-like, although that was the excuse she had made to Belle, but simply because she had an instinctive shrinking from doing so.

Well, the material did not need to cost a lot. She did not want to be overdressed, but on the other hand she did not want to present a 'poor little governess' image. She wanted to show them that pale English girls could vie with Outback lasses. But a sudden look in the mirror showed her that she was no longer pale. Glenn should see her and also should admire her.

They were inside the Ali Baba cave, where behind louvred thickly-shaded show windows there were bales of every imaginable material that anyone had ever dreamed of—nylons; polyester in gay tinges; pure silks which made her mouth water; muslins; cottons in every colour; Indian silks with gold threadwork around the edges.

'I could spend forever here,' said Jill dreamily, fingering a scarlet cotton.

'I could spend here forever,' corrected the older girl.

Jill stared. 'That's what I said. Oh, I get it—grammar.'

'Grammar,' agreed Aline gravely, and thought she could spend every cent she had got and had not got in this shop, but did not say so.

What she finally did buy was white broderie anglaise, a sensible cotton which did not look sensible at all, a soft, slithery thing which would make a gorgeous pants-suit and which could be prettied up with ribbons—silver ribbons, scarlet ribbons, golden ribbons.

Ribbons as golden as dreams.

'Yes, we did have needlecraft at school,' said Jill, reverting to their previous conversation and running her fingers through a pile of inexpensive remnants. 'But I didn't like Mrs Watson, and anyhow, the things the girls made were never very interesting. Not like yours.'

'I didn't make all my things,' objected Aline. 'And I could teach you to sew, Jill, if you really want to. Would you like to try to make a sun frock? We'll ask your father, shall we?'

A lower lip was pushed forward. 'I've got enough pocket money to buy some material,' the younger girl said mutinously. 'And I want to choose it. I don't want Belle to thrust her sticky fingers into everything.'

'Belle's very nice,' said Aline.

'You think so?' Jill replied without a smile. 'Do you mean you'll show me, or do you have to ask Dad?'

'Oh, I'll teach you all right. But as for buying the material—look, Jill, I can't let you spend your pocket money on things like clothing without asking Bill, but I'll buy the cotton for you. Don't worry, it's not expensive.'

'You're crazy,' said Jill, but she hugged Aline.

So the sewing machine was pulled near the window and the two girls spent every moment of Aline's free time running up seams, fitting and putting together, laughing and admiring, and Jill quite forgot that she did not really like having a 'governess'.

Jill was a quick learner and the sun frock grew amazingly fast. The pants-suit took shape under Aline's slim fingers, and even Belle admired it. The choice of ribbons necessitated another visit to the township, and this time it was Bill who took them as well as the twins.

'You can't go in there with your sticky fingers,' said Jill to the twins in true elder-sister fashion. 'Look, Aline, you pop in and I'll keep an eye on them, don't worry.' She tried to sound very grown-up and responsible.

Aline did hesitate for a moment, but the shop entrance was wide and she could keep them under her eye, so she thanked Jill and tried not to look too relieved when Bill, who had been talking to an acquaintance, finished the conversation, and coming up, decided it was time for afternoon tea. 'If you can eat anything after that ice-cream,' he told the twins.

The little girls gurgled ecstatically at the thought of more sticky messes such as cream cakes, ice-creams and similar goodies.

Jill slipped in after Aline. 'I'm coming with you.'

Silver, gold and scarlet—amethyst, garnet red, aquamarine, colours with names as lovely and romantic as frankincense and myrrh. Colours as lovely as the blare of the trumpets at some ancient tournament, when the knights rode gaily into the skirmish, brandishing on shimmering lances their ladies' favours.

'Gold—oh, please, gold,' begged Jill, fingering a shimmering ribbon.

'That red——' Aline hesitated, squeezing her eyes shut and wishing she had brought the almost finished pants-suit with her, but she had not thought it of importance because, after all, white was white. However, now it seemed so difficult to decide.

'What about these?' asked the shop owner. From one hand she trailed a conglomeration of silver ribbons—silver velvet and silver satin and silver lace.

'Beautiful, aren't they?' she said, sounding genuine.

'This,' Jill decided, picking with unerring taste a narrow silver ribbon, etched velvet, soft as a dream. 'For the neckline—and maybe the pockets. And you could get a second colour for other times, this one here.'

So the ribbons were wrapped and they went and had had tea and Aline ate just as much as the children, which was quite a feast, and they had a very happy time. Aline looked at Bill's attentive face, in its way so reminiscent of Glenn.

The thought of Glenn brought her back to realities. Glenn would soon be coming. He would hear about the dam débâcle and probably think her a fool. He was not likely to be impressed by her seat on a horse, and would laugh at her Outback lass act. He's even going to find it unusual that I sit with the family in the evenings, she thought. He's going to spoil everything, and any softness I remember is just my imagination—a wish dream and making myself a fool's paradise to live in.

The moon went away—and the thunder growled, and the white pants-suit on its hanger awaited the morning and its completion. Aline found herself wanting it to be morning, so that

Glenn would be here. After all, nothing much could happen, as long as she kept her head.

Bill and Belle went to Brisbane to pick up Glenn. Bill had invited Aline, who had found an excuse not to go. The reason, she knew, was that she was daunted by the thought of meeting Glenn. Jill was sulking because she had wanted to go and the twins were making as much trouble as they could.

'Libby, darling, don't pull at the curtain, it'll come down.'

The little blonde paid no attention.

'Libby, did you hear me? Look, darling, here's Teddy. Let's play with him.'

The little girl pouted.

'Libby, come here at once!' The old-fashioned tone of authority which practice had taught her helped. The little girl left the ill-treated curtain alone, but not before she had torn a hole in the thin nylon. 'Oh, dear,' shrugged Aline, thinking of Belle and her lifted eyebrows.

'I don't want to work, I'm too hot,' Jill announced. 'Aline, let's do some sewing.'

The thought of a bit of peace and quiet, with the twins playing on the veranda and—she hoped—being good, was tempting. And

Christmas was coming and sewing lessons, after all, were lessons.

'Oh, all right,' conceded Aline, pushing books away. 'Twins, come on, we're going out on to the patio.'

Their yells, first of pleasure, then in play, showed her she had been too optimistic as far as peace and quiet were concerned. And it was far too hot for words, or for eating or for anything barring a cold drink and her cool bed. Aline had never experienced heat quite like this.

'Blast!' exclaimed Jill, grabbing a twin. 'You did that, you horrible brat, you!' Orange juice was cascading in a yellow sticky stream over her jeans and shirt, and over Aline's too.

And just then Bill and Belle and Glenn came walking up to the house, the plane's arrival having been unobserved in the noise. And the quartet that faced the immaculate two men and one woman was hot and tear-stained—and in Aline's case white with a temper she had not known she possessed.

So much for her dream of presenting to Glenn a picture of a soignée, sun-tanned, sure-of-herself girl who coped with children, climate and climaxes without a lift of her eyebrows.

'Oh, no, not again,' That was Belle, her well-cut dress clinging in all those spots where a well-cut dress ought to cling, her hair loose and pretty, her eyes full of amusement. 'Bill, really, nobody can cope with those brats of yours! I can't, and no girl born of woman can. Poor Aline!'

'Accidents will happen,' grinned Bill. 'And we aren't that low on water. Get into the bathroom, you horrible children, you. And Jill, I'd expect you to have a bit more sense.'

Jill was indignant. 'I didn't do it. It was Libby or Nan who pushed over the glass. What am I supposed to do? It's not fair! It isn't fair!'

Aline was only too aware of Glenn's presence. Here was the perfect opportunity to show her poise, to smile sweetly, say how do you do, and whisk the children off without childish explanations or apologies or complaints, but instead she found herself staring at the wide shoulders, the arrogant profile, the sudden— was it a shadow of laughter?—in Glenn's eyes and see derision there, where quite possibly only laughter was meant to be. She flared, just as hotly as Jill had done. 'And this just confirms what you've been thinking all the time, doesn't it, Mr Jennings? Unfit to work in a shop, unfit to look after your nieces. Good evening!' She grabbed the twins' hands and disappeared into the darkened room, with loud wails from incensed tots as they went.

That evening the candles flared on the table, the place mats were modern and beautiful, as was the crockery and the cutlery. The fare was not complicated. She found that Outback stations did not go in for sauces and pâtés and bits and pieces of sophisticated city eating. There was iced soup; there were underdone steaks and a tossed salad; there was a sweet which combined fruit, ice-cream and sherried biscuits. Aline suddenly found herself wishing she had put on her best dress. As a matter of fact, she had put it on, but had then taken it off and worn something plainer. She was not going to dress up for him. She would have liked to, but she was not going to let Glenn think that she had done so.

The big wall mirror showed a girl with flushed cheeks and silver hair, damp amethyst eyes and lace-like lashes.

'You don't eat enough to keep alive,' said Bill, who had made that remark many times before. But then there had been no Glenn there, and that had made all the difference. Now Aline's lashes flew up, her lips hardened and she observed, she knew unreasonably, 'I don't do this, I don't do that, Bill, and I don't do the rest. Why don't you sack me, and have done with it?'

'Probably too scared of you,' said Glenn, almost indulgently. This was a new Glenn, urbane and relaxed, something which she had not experienced before. She felt caught at a disadvantage.

She reacted boorishly as though she was talking to the Glenn she had known in the past. 'I'm not scared of you,' she said. 'Not any more. I realise that nothing I do is right—never has been with you. I don't ride well enough, I don't swim well enough and obviously I don't manage the children properly. Not to your satisfaction.'

'Who said so?' grinned Bill.

'Your brother.'

'Up to now I haven't opened my mouth,' Glenn said easily. She felt his eyes upon her.

Aline knew she had been caught on the wrong foot and had reacted boorishly. 'You don't need to speak,' she said crossly. 'You just need to look.'

Belle interposed tactfully, 'Even a cat can look at a king.'

'At a king, yes,' said Glenn, that indulgent note still in his voice. 'But not at our Miss Mel-

lan. She thinks it's what old-fashioned officers
used to call 'dumb insolence' in the ranks . . .
If you feel so miserable, Miss Mellan, why
don't you go and lie down? It's hot enough to
make anyone cross.'

If it was not a conciliatory speech it certainly
was not aggressive, unless she was determined
to take it so. Aline had been expecting a different approach from this new indulgent Glenn
and found it hard to handle the situation. She
rose and said coolly, 'I have been invited to
spend my evenings with the family. Now that
you're here I won't presume to do so. And perhaps you'd like me to take my meals in the
kitchen if the cook does not object.'

'It's usually a tray in her room for the governess,' agreed Glenn, and Aline could not help
but feel he was laughing at her and that she
deserved it. 'Only the cook might object to
that.'

Aline whirled out of the room.

And the battle continued next morning.

She had made up her mind to keep out of
Glenn's way as much as possible and not to
commit herself. But she had reckoned without
Jill. The men trooped in next morning and, as
usual, Bill wished her, 'Good morning, Aline,
except that it's not cool enough to be one. Hor-

rible! I wouldn't be surprised if we had a thunderstorm.'

'I can do with a cup of coffee,' sighed Belle, coming in from outside. 'Good morning, Aline. Did you sleep? I felt as if I was having a sauna bath without even trying!'

Aline was very conscious of Glenn, watching for him to speak.

'Good morning, Miss Mellan,' he said punctiliously. 'Good morning, children.'

'Why don't you call her Aline, as we all do?' demanded Jill, looking up from her bacon and eggs. 'We're friendly in the Outback.'

Glenn looked down at her from his six-foot-two whip-slenderness. 'Mind your own business, young lady.'

Aline was glad when they were at their lessons. She was glad when the men did not return for their lunch.

But she was aggrieved when they did not come in for the evening meal, and only returned once the twins were in bed and Jill was reading preparatory to switching out her light—or having it switched out on her. They were tired-looking and grimed with the flying dust of the plains, hot from the windy ride in the jeep. Bill waved his hand at her, 'If I don't get a drink soon I'll die, and the funeral had better be immediately,' and he disappeared into the house. Glenn looked at her, a long look which she could not understand. Tenderness—it could not be that. Friendliness it certainly was not. What was it? Arrogance, thought Aline, clinging to her preconceptions, however wrongly. When he went in she burst into tears, huddling in the cane chair, weeping silently into the hot cushions with their smell of crushed and withering wistaria, of Belle's expensive perfume and the children's earth-stained sandals, the twins considering chairs a proper medium to be stood on rather than sat in.

Some nightbird cried in the distance and once again the moon was red. Some night creatures scuffled in the arid grass, and the breeze seemed straight from hell.

'I wish I was back in England,' thought Aline, remembering the wide green sweep of the moors where she and some friends had once gone for a walking tour, of the craggy tors, of the Downs near Brighton and the vivid splash of the sea. Of London with its mists and its sunshine and rain and the statues standing as they had done down the centuries. Piccadilly Circus and its milling crowd of humanity. Knightsbridge with its boutiques where she and her friends had window-shopped, wondering whether they would ever be able to afford some of the very highly priced items displayed. Hyde Park and the busy traffic bustling. A stretch of pale blue or grey sky over the gay purlieus of Hampstead Heath. And of course, it should have been Jim. But Jim was nothing but a pale puppet now, someone of no importance, a child's fancy, blown away by the heat of reality. Someone else had taken his place.

'Aline!' A tall figure emerged from the darkness. Her heart began to thump. But it wasn't Glenn, it was Bill.

'Aline,' he said again, and took her into his arms. It was not the first time that he had so held her, and nothing had been serious about it before, and nothing was serious about it now, except that his light kiss felt the sting of Aline's tears. And what he might have said then, or done then, or how he might have reacted, would never be known, because Glenn suddenly loomed up.

Just for a moment his eyes caught hers, and she saw in them that old contemptuous look. His words matched his looks. 'Still prospecting, Miss Gold-digger,' he said drily, and immediately vanished in the darkness.

Aline ran back into the house. The twins were engrossed in one of their boisterous games and Jill fortunately was absent, when Bill way-laid her.

'Aline . . . ' He sounded like Glenn. 'You aren't really leaving?'

Aline muttered that she had no choice.

'Look, you're employed by me; at least, you're teaching my children. The twins love you and even Jill seems to have taken to you. Please, Aline! I know Glenn's rather nose-in-the-air and has ideals as high as a skyscraper, but since that blasted Marlene two-timed him with his best friend a month before the wedding he hasn't got a good word to say to any female, although I'll admit he seems specially set against you. But you're partly to blame. You start to scrap, and your addiction to Mrs Delamaine doesn't help. Marlene's related to her and she engineered the whole thing, and he was head-over-heels, till he found her out, but even then Mrs Delamaine never forgave him. Anyhow, you'll stay, won't you?'

In her heart Aline knew she was going to stay. She told herself it was because there was a lot of unemployment, because she had to save money for her fare back to England and because she was sorry for Jill, who was such an outsider. But she knew those were not the reasons. The only reason was that she loved

Glenn. She might have to fool the world; she was not going to fool herself.

She loved Glenn, not with the light amusement which Bill provided, not with the romantic being-in-love sentiment she had felt for Jim, but with the one and only love of a lifetime.

She did not want to love him. She hated to do so. She could think of nothing worse—except never to see him again, never to hear the sting of his words, never to feel the casual brush of his hand as he passed sugar or salt or bread.

And she stared at the sky brassy and brash over the lash of the wind and the scurrying over the clouds, and wished she did not have to face the fact that her Glenn was never going to regard her as anything but a nuisance and a gold-digger.

CHAPTER EIGHT

HER ROOM was nicely furnished, but the only mirror was not floor-length. Usually it quite sufficed, but with her pants-suit finished to the last bit of appliquéd embroidery, Aline wanted to see herself from all sides. Fortunately the lounge boasted a mirror wall. So the morning before the party, Aline, finding sleep difficult, got up very early and padded through the corridors and into that room.

The rest of the family was still fast asleep and there was not even a sound from the twins. In the east a faint tinge of sun coloured the arid earth and caught itself in the fronds of the palms. There were some clouds in the sky, but Aline, who with the other members of the household had got into the habit of staring hopefully at them and wondering whether the promise of rain would this time be fulfilled, paid no attention to them now, except to hope that the picnic would not be spoiled by the weather, a wish every farmer would have hated her for. But economic conditions or not, future food supplies or not, she had only one thing on her mind.

The blinds were still drawn, but she jerked them up and let in every bit of sunlight. She pirouetted before the mirror, then stood stock still, looking at herself. The white broderie anglaise pant-suit was perfect to the last stitch—the beautifully embroidered blouse just frilly enough, the ribbons the last touch of glamour. Her silver-fair hair was loose around her narrow cheeks and her usually disciplined mouth half open as if to suck from life every last trace of sweetness. Silver sandals emphasised the silver lacquer of her toenails.

Aline stared at herself almost in disbelief. 'This isn't me!' she gasped. 'Why, I'm different!'

Then, before she could think further, a pair of arms went round her and she found herself embraced.

'Oh, stop it, do, Bill!' snapped Aline impatiently, trying to twist herself loose. She had something better to do than to pay attention to Bill's shenanigans. The arms around her tightened and she felt herself turned round. The man in whose arms she was—from whose grasp she could not break—was Glenn. For just a moment she thought she saw in his eyes a look she had never seen there before, a look almost of tenderness.

A long moment they stood there, so close that she could see the flecks in his eyes and the tiny silken hairs of his eyebrows. She could feel the beating of his heart—and then she could not, for her own was racing in reply.

Her dry lips tried to say his name. Her lips moistened with desire, but she could not speak.

And then it was too late. That unfathomable look left his face. 'So that's how it is!' he blazed at her. 'So that's how it's been between Bill and you!' His eyes were rock-hard in the pallor of his face. 'All tucked up here conveniently together, and never mind Belle and her feelings!' The flare of anger intensified. 'Do you know that Bill has very little money, and what he has he needs for his children? Do you know that it's not worth your while to fool him, only to drop him later on when you meet someone who has more? Bill's a fool who doesn't realise what you are, which even that idiot of a Mrs Delamaine does. Do you care even a bit that he and Belle were as good as engaged until you came?'

Aline whispered, 'Mrs Delamaine?'

'Yes, Mrs Delamaine. Do you think she too would fall for your gold-digging, as Gran did?

Why, Mrs Delamaine can't stand me, never mind why, but even so she warned me before you came. Warned me not to be duped by you, told me how Gran had sent you money and sent you presents and had finally sent you the permit when you . . . Oh, I know you never actually *asked*. You were always the brave little girl who was fighting to keep herself, all alone in a hard world. You just hinted and hinted, and Gran fell for it. With all her sense Gran was an easy touch.'

'But I still felt we owed you something, for bringing you out. I thought about what she'd said. I didn't believe her at first, but why should Mrs Delamaine lie? Oh, she'd do it at the drop of a hat, and more easily than that if she would benefit, but she had nothing more to gain. Nothing to gain, so . . . I still thought I'd pay you to go back and see that you were all right. Even when you came . . . well, I was fighting against wanting to believe you. Your saying you didn't want to accept anything. Your pretending you didn't want my money, our money, that you were going to pay it all back.' He broke off.

Then he resumed, while Aline listened in frozen silence.

'You went and crawled to Mrs Delamaine for a frock. Not for the fare back to England or to get you a job, but for a bit of . . . of rubbish. You wanted that—that finery so much that you pushed aside whatever pride you had, and pleaded with her. Our Mrs Delamaine isn't an easy touch, but she bought it for you. She told you you'd have no use for it on a station— but you told her you wanted a husband and that in the Outback there were supposed to be bachelors, and . . . She didn't think you meant Bill and she was sorry for you. Yes, even a hard piece like Mrs Delamaine was sorry for you, and indignant that we kept you so short. But she came to her senses and she told me.'

The thought of Mrs Delamaine and her lies flashed through Aline's mind. Why had she lied? Why did she hate me so much? she thought. What have I done to her that she hated me so much? And Bill. And Belle. Bill never even looked at Belle. Belle was not interested in him. If she had been, why had she asked Aline to stay? She *had* asked her.

Had she not been so shattered by Glenn's words, Aline might have replied. She might have been able to voice her bewilderment and her indignation. As it was, she could not say anything.

She blinked to force back her tears, looked at him for what seemed a long time and then, pulling herself loose, ran without looking where she was going and so full tilt into Bill's arms, and when he said soothingly, 'Whoa, whoa, then,' as if speaking to a startled horse, she gasped, 'Glenn, it's Glenn!' and burst into tears.

'You know, Glenn, this has to stop,' said Bill. 'You might just as well get used to having Aline around, because we're going to be married.'

Aline, open-mouthed and still tear-stained, did not deny it. There was too much anger and love and frustration in her heart for that. Yes, and utter misery as she stared at Glenn's face. Of course she was not going to marry Bill. Bill did not really want her. He had said what he had said because it was the best way out of an awkward situation. He no more loved her than she loved him. But why shouldn't they teach Glenn a lesson?

She did not want to think about Mrs Delamaine and what Mrs Delamaine had said, if she *had* said it. That was too puzzling and too cruel. But Bill and Belle—that made no sense. Was Belle in love with Bill? Had she spoiled something for Belle? Could that calm soignée woman have hidden her feelings so well? Were the occasional flashes of sharply-curbed anger or dislike really signs that Belle was suffering because she thought Bill and Aline were enjoying a flirtation?

Aline shook her head and tried to push the thought away. There was so much she would have to consider, but this was not the time for it. She was too busy with the last-minute preparations for the picnic. And also, Belle or no Belle, Mrs Delamaine or no Mrs Delamaine, and Glenn and Bill, or no Glenn and Bill, she was going to enjoy herself, and nobody was going to stop her. Not even her own treacherous heart.

Lunch sensibly was cold, chicken with slices of tomatoes, green peppers, white spring onions, yellow lemons nestling inside lettuce and then an ice-cream dessert which would have pleased a gourmet. But Belle just picked at her food, complained that the chicken was too dry, the ice-cream not eatable, and that she really ought to be in bed and get rid of her headache.

'Do lie down,' urged Aline. 'We've got nearly everything ready, and Jill and I can do the last bits and pieces.'

'I really think I will. These nasty migraines,' said the older woman, and stood up. For a moment she almost lost her balance, but she waved aside every offer of help and tottered rather than walked out of the room.

'Auntie sick,' said Nan with satisfaction. 'Very sick Auntie.'

'More biks,' agreed her twin, who also knew it was easier to get around Aline than Auntie Belle.

'Horrid children!' reprimanded Aline. 'Poor Auntie. And stop grinning like the Cheshire Cat, Jill. A migraine headache's nasty.'

'Aline, what's a Cheshire Cat? I always wondered. I asked Daddy but he didn't seem to know. Do you?'

Aline shook her head. 'Finish your ice-cream, Jill. I want to get the twins ready for their nap, and get on with the preparations.'

But Aline was not destined to be allowed to do so, for just as she was folding paper napkins into attractive shapes the little lubra who helped in the kitchen came running in, big beautiful eyes wide in her brown face. 'Belle, Mrs Belle—she sick. All over everything, and talking funny.'

Aline dropped the serviettes and ran.

Belle was semi-conscious, retching and moaning. On her bedside table stood a jug of lemonade and an empty medicine bottle—a bottle that had contained sleeping pills. She was obviously in desperate straits.

'Get the doctor,' said Aline to the little lubra. 'Quick! Or tell Cook to get him and you run and tell Mr Bill.'

But at that moment Glenn strode in, small beads of perspiration on his forehead, his shirt crumpled. His lips thinned as he took in the sick woman and the chaos around her. 'Coffee,' he snapped, and the little lubra panted, 'I'll get it quick,' and ran.

The next hour was like something Aline never wanted to experience again. They poured coffee into Belle's unresponsive mouth, forced her to stand upright and walked her up and down the room, talking to her, trying to stop her from drooping, from sleeping. Outside, a few lances of rain danced against the window panes and thunder rumbled somewhere far away. Jill, white-faced, drifted in and out and sensibly brought fresh relays of coffee. Bill arrived at the same time as the doctor and stared at Belle with horror.

'Well, the worst is over,' said the doctor cheerfully. 'But we have a very sick girl here.

Silly to keep sleeping draughts next to the bed. Take one, become drowsy, forget you took one and hey presto! Come on, Belle, drink this—and here's something else that will help you.' He filled the disposable syringe and Belle flinched. 'Won't hurt,' he told her, still keeping up the cheerful patter.

'I'll call off the picnic,' said Bill. 'Gastric 'flu, I think it had better be.'

During the evening Glenn asked Aline to come into the office. He looked tired, with the sheen of utter weariness beneath the tan of his face. 'Please sit down, Miss Mellan,' he invited.

'I prefer to stand,' said Aline, although she would have loved to sit.

'I won't take long. And I don't like to say what I have to. We haven't got on from the beginning, and that doesn't make this any easier,' said Glenn. His voice was weary too. 'Please believe that this has nothing to do with what I said earlier on about Mrs Delamaine. She isn't a very truthful woman. I think she spoke the truth this time, but anyhow, it doesn't affect the outcome. I think you'll understand that, while I don't say the reason for Belle taking all those pills is your fault, it's still necessary for you to leave here immediately and return to England. I'll get the seat, give you six months' salary in lieu of notice and pay your hotel bill until there's a vacancy on a plane.'

'I'll leave here and immediately, but I'm not going back to England,' said Aline firmly.

'As I said, I'm not blaming you for Belle's actions. If you're going to say, as you obviously mean to, that she was being neurotic I'll even agree. But I'm fond of Belle and I have a duty to her. As long as you're in Australia, the relationship between you and Bill will not end, and end it must. I'm sorry, Miss Mellan, but for Belle's sake and for Bill's, I have to insist.'

'No,' repeated Aline. 'I'm leaving. But it's up to me to say where I'm going and what I do.' She heard her own stubborn voice with surprise.

Glenn got up from the chair on the edge of which he had been perching and leaned over her. 'All right, then. If you won't go I can't make you. But I won't have Bill's life spoiled, or the children's. And I won't have Belle made unhappy. Do you understand? I know you're going to say that if Bill loves Belle he could have said so. I think you underestimate your own charm. I know you'll say Belle doesn't get on with the children, that she won't make them a good mother. She isn't fond of children, I'll

agree, but once she and Bill are married she'll
be happier, and being happier she'll be nicer to
them and when they're her own she'll love
them. And also—forgive me, but it's really
none of your business.'

'And it's none of your business what I do
with my own life! And your saying "forgive" is
only an empty phrase, which you don't mean.'

'That's true,' Glenn shrugged.

'Do you really believe, even for a moment,
any of my statement? Right, then I'll tell you
something else that's true. I did *not* ask Mrs
Delamaine for the dress. I did not—as I've said
before—ask your grandmother for any presents, money or otherwise. I did not sponge and
I did not crawl. And . . . '

'Miss Mellan, I don't believe you, though I
should like to. But let's drop this—it's imma-
terial. We aren't talking about gifts and dresses:
we're talking about a family, my family, and
about life. So if you're still determined to marry
Bill, here's another proposition. I don't like
you; I don't trust you,' again there was that
curious tremor in his voice, 'but I'm willing to
marry you—if I have to in order to get your
fingers off Bill. And I'm a much better match
than he is and I can give you all those things
you want—money, a beautiful home, jewels

and gowns and a position as one of Melbourne's foremost hostesses. And——' his voice was grim '—I'll admit that, actress that you are, you'll be able to fill your position well. So all you have to do now is to make up your mind. Marry me or——' he hesitated briefly and his voice was almost pleading '—go back to London, Aline, and pick up the threads of your life and put the time here behind you as part of a nightmare.'

Her lips opened to say, 'I'm going home,' but what came out was something different. 'I haven't got a choice, have I?'

'I'm giving you a choice.' His voice was dry, rasping, and his eyes did not meet hers.

'No choice.' she insisted, having to say something.

'No choice at all,' he agreed, 'if you're sensible. And I'm just thinking—if you'd like to go to the Casino in Tasmania or have a bit of a fling at Surfers Paradise I'll pay for that too. You haven't had too good a time here. Just one of those things.'

He could not have said anything worse.

'Just one of those things,' echoed her heart, and she swallowed her tears.

Glenn's eyes were on her, hard eyes, questioning eyes, eyes that asked something to

which she had no answer, and she ought to
have it. The answer which would be the key to
untangling the mess they had jointly made. The
key to bliss. If she could only find it, Bill, Belle
and Mrs Delamaine notwithstanding, things
might still come out all right. She searched desperately in the tangles of her mind, but there
was nothing but an utter emptiness which
appalled her, or would have done had she been
able to think. But she could not think. She just
wanted to be in his arms.

So all right. What was it Bill had said—
Glenn's fiancée had two-timed him, and that
had hurt and embittered him. But that was no
excuse. Jim had two-timed and left her, and she
was not bitter.

But if he had really loved the girl, that Marlene who was a relation of Mrs Delamaine, it
was a different matter. Aline herself had not
really loved Jim, so there was no comparison.

She tried. 'I'm not out for what I can get. I'm
not wanting a holiday in Surfers Paradise or
anywhere.'

But Glenn was not looking at her any more;
he was watching the ceiling as if he had never
seen one before. 'I'm leaving for Melbourne
tomorrow, and I'll be back for the picnic. You
can stay here and give me your decision then.

I'm not rushing you.' For a moment he faced her again. For a moment she thought his voice was soft and his eyes were tender. But then he walked out of the room, leaving behind him the open drawers of the desk, the untidy heap of papers he had been reading and the ash tray littered with Bill's cigarettes.

Reality was a steady ache in her heart, a dull mind and the knowledge that she could not win. If she married Glenn, she would have the joy of his company, but she would also have the knowledge that he despised her more than ever, and in those circumstances how could she actually enjoy his company, however much she loved him? If she left—well, she would have lost him for ever. But he was lost to her anyhow, if you can talk of 'losing' someone you have never had.

She made up her mind to leave, tell him that yes, she would go to Melbourne or Sydney, while he arranged for her to fly out of Australia and then to vanish. Once she was out of his life—and what was more important to him, out of Bill's life—he would not look for her and she would at least have saved the last tattered remnants of her pride.

And once she had decided, she grimly got on with the business of the day, because while

everything within her shrieked for the relief of
running away immediately, she was not going
to slink out, leaving Bill and Belle in the lurch.
She was going to stay and do her work, then
leave quietly. A week or so was not endless.

CHAPTER NINE

THE CHRISTMAS tree flamed in the artificially darkened room. The twins drew deep breaths of delight and threw chubby arms around everyone's neck, lisping something or other about Father Christmas. Christmas fare loaded down the tables, Belle and Bill were sparring happily as they had done before the débâcle and, obviously, whatever had caused Belle to take those pills had nothing to do with Bill. According to her, she had become drowsy and must have taken too many tablets.

'I can't take that, Bill,' protested Aline, having thanked Jill for the dressing table runner of Indian muslin, and having hugged the twins for the box of chocolates which obviously their father had bought for them to give to her and which obviously they had every intention of eating themselves. She had also thanked Belle for the scent. She now held the little box in her hands and stared at the brilliant-cut diamond ring, which sparkled and gleamed. 'This . . . this . . .'

'It's really not a Christmas present,' said Bill, half apologetically. 'It's our engagement ring. I should have given it to you before or afterwards, but I only got it yesterday and I couldn't wait to see your face. Your Christmas presents,' he waved towards a conglomeration of parcels on the table, 'are over there.'

'But Bill,' she protested, wanting to say, 'Well, you know our engagement was only and is only a humbug to annoy Glenn, and you must know that the need for even that is past. And this—this is proper jewellery, not make believe.' But it was difficult to say things like that in front of an interested Jill and noisy twins, and most of all, Belle.

She looked at the older woman, a fleeting glance, and something turned in her heart. Because Glenn had not said it just to hurt her. Belle did love Bill. Only for a second had the haggard shadow rested on that serene face, but it was enough. Pain such as that should not be suffered for any reason, and certainly not for makebelieve. She said, 'Bill——' urgently, but Belle had already left the room and the children claimed her time. She would have to wait for the evening.

But before then Glenn came back, earlier than expected, and took the first opportunity to face her, in the empty lounge.

'Congratulations,' he grated.

Puzzled, Aline deliberately struck a light note. 'Congratulations? It's not my birthday. And I haven't achieved anything—I mean passed an exam or . . . '

'My congratulations,' he explained, 'for being the world's most accomplished gold-digger. I thought I had your measure, but I was wrong.'

Hurt and heat flared up in her. 'I'm tired of being called a gold-digger! I'm tired of being—being told off. I've explained until I'm sick of it that I never asked your grandmother for anything. What she gave, she gave because she wanted to, and I could have asked for more and she would have given that too, but I never did. Do you understand? I never did! Maybe I don't talk your sort of language, maybe I'm not making myself clear. But that's how it is.'

His face did not soften; if such a thing was possible it even grew harder. 'And you're well repaid for your restraint, Miss Aline Mellan. Stop looking so innocent. Stop flushing so innocently. Don't pretend you didn't know about Gran's will. She didn't just leave you a couple of thousand dollars or a nice piece of jewellery, but an expensive unit in the best part of Melbourne, shares worth a fortune, and a large sum of money on top of it. You ought to open a school for spongers, and whatever fee you cared to charge would be worth it!'

Aline looked at him in astonishment as he continued, 'When Mrs Delamaine started to warn me—yes, as soon as we knew the exact date of your arrival, I was wondering whether she was just trying to make trouble between Gran and me. Because Mrs Delamaine always blamed me for the break-up between Marlene and myself. Apparently I was supposed to take—anyhow, that's none of your business. When I started to show interest in you and she realised it, even if you didn't, I wondered whether she was just trying to get you out of the way. She always wanted Marlene and me— but again, it's none of your business. I tried to fight against starting to believe in your pictured innocence, and like a fool I nearly fell for it. But this . . . Look here, Miss Mellan, I— we—we wouldn't have grudged you a nice little something—we probably would have sent you something pretty substantial if we'd never met you. As it is, I'll fight you. It will cost me more in lawyers' fees than you're worth, but I'll do it and like it.'

'For a principle,' suggested the girl who looked like Aline, but who spoke as Aline under natural circumstances would not have spoken.

'For a principle,' he grated. 'So—get yourself packed and get out. I'll fly you to Brisbane but I won't have you in the house. You—you aren't the sort of person I want here, nor will Bill when he comes to his senses.'

'And you stick so closely to upright principles, don't you?' Aline replied.

'I do,' he said, no change in his voice or eyes or manner.

'Which is why you offered to marry me, despite the fact that you neither like nor love me, just to keep your hands on that bit of family property your grandmother willed to me.'

It was a blow beneath the belt, doubly unfair because Aline realised that he would not have known of the bequest when he had offered her marriage. Had he known he would have told her then. It was a blow in the solar plexus. His lips tightened for a moment.

And then finally he spoke, after a moment or an eternity, while the web of misunderstanding thickened. The sun glared through the chinks in the blind and wove patterns on the etched coldness of his face.

'Not because of the money, whatever you think. Not because of envy, whatever you feel. Not even because of Bill. He's not a baby—let him dree his own weird. Not because of Belle, fond though I am of her. But because of love for you, Miss Aline Mellan, who's so busy climbing ladders to success and security that she doesn't bother to look where she treads or on whom. Because I couldn't bear to see you in Bill's arms. For my own sake. Because while I didn't respect you I was searching for reasons which would have changed my mind—allowed me to change it. Because I didn't like what I saw in you, but I told myself that life had hurt you and maybe somehow I could alter you, change you back into what you'd once been or what you would have been had you had a happier childhood. Because I loved you so much that I was willing to accept you anyhow on any conditions, let you despise, dislike me, hate me, as long as I could hold you in my arms, and close my eyes and feel you near my heart. What do I say—in my heart? And I'm not in the habit of making flowery speeches, so you'll see how low you've brought me. But this—this I can't take. It's not the money, it's the slyness, the calculated slyness.'

He turned, his hands held out before him like a blind man, and flung at her, 'You sheltered under our roof. You pretended love for Bill and for his children. You lured him away from Belle and you—you feigned all the time that you didn't know!' And the echo of his footsteps died in the distance.

The little lubra, in her Christmas finery, slipped into the room and handed Aline a big official envelope. Aline opened it with frozen fingers and read that the Chief Nursing Officer who had promised to contact her former Sister Tutor was now offering her a place in her next intake of trainees. Aline wired her acceptance, determined to leave immediately after the party. Not that she was in a party mood, but she could not, would not, leave everyone, the twins, Bill, and most of all a red-eyed Jill in the lurch. Since the girl had heard that she had to return to school at the beginning of the new school year she had been in a strange mood, but Bill only laughed and said she would have to get used to it.

So Aline dressed the twins who were trotting after her ecstatically and admired Jill in her party finery and made her smile just for a moment and tried to console her. Then she dressed herself in her pants-suit with the silver ribbons, in her frilly blouse with its silver bows and its silver embroidery into each stitch of which she had put so much effort. She brushed her almost-silver-fair hair and combed it up high with the aid of a silver comb Belle had lent her. And she told herself that in less than one day and night she would be on her way. She would fly to Melbourne. She would see the solicitor whose name Glenn had let fall and she would tell him that she wanted none of her legacy, with the exception of a small sum sufficient to tide her over the next weeks until her training began, and that even that she would regard as a loan. And she would wrap the Jennings and their doings into heavy rolls of whatever material served best to aid forgetfulness.

It was a party to end all parties, with laughing people, lively music, lovely clothes and high spirits. The food was wonderful. Belle looked like a fashion model. The twins were being cuddled by everyone and—more important to them—had titbits thrust into ever-willing mouths, not of food suitable to their age, but bits of caviar on toast, and meringues smothered in whipped cream and brandy.

'They're starting young,' smiled Bill, obviously unperturbed.

'I'm not going back to school,' said Jill, seeking help from the neighbours, all of whom assured her that they had felt exactly as she did, but once they were there had loved school, which was hardly convincing to Jill, bearing in mind her history of running away from school.

After the party the family listened to the late news. Bush fires had been burning not far from the property as Outback people reckon distances, but now they were coming nearer. Both Glenn and Bill were in the Voluntary Fire Brigade and had orders to stand by.

The lights went out, the moon took over and silence reigned. Aline, sleepless with tension and worry, sat up as she heard the motor rev up and the men leave. 'Oh, Glenn! Glenn . . . '

The children were fractious in the morning, and Aline and even Belle did their best to entertain them. By mutual consent they had let Jill sleep. It was the best possible thing for the unhappy little girl—or so they thought.

But about eleven o'clock, when Aline had almost decided to go into her room, a car braked violently in front of the house and a frantic neighbour hurtled inside. 'Jill . . . Diane . . . Are they here?'

'Jill's asleep,' said Belle blankly. 'She's overtired.'

For answer, Mrs Martin, who knew the place well, ran through the corridor into Jill's room and held the door wide open. 'Just see!'

The bed was empty, the sheets thrown back. Some clothes had been pulled out of the drawers, which gaped wide open. On the dresser-table there was a note.

'Like mine,' said Mrs Martin. 'Oh, don't waste time. They've gone—to Jill's former nurse. Running away because Jill doesn't want to go to school, and my fool daughter helped her. And the woman lives—oh, heavens, Belle, you know better than I do! Right past the bush fire area.'

'What are we standing here for?' demanded Belle. 'I'm going. No, Aline, you stay here. Someone has got to, and you don't know the place. We don't want to have to send out search parties for you.' She hurried out of the house, across to Mrs Martin's small car. Mrs Martin followed her and they vanished into the grey smoke-laden landscape.

An hour crawled slowly past. 'Those poor silly children,' whispered the old cook. The twins huddled close to Aline.

Belle's right, she thought. I don't know the place, I'll never find them. I'm a new chum, so I'd only be a liability. But something rose inside her, something stronger than fear or sense, than reasoning, something maternal, loving, primitive as earth and as enduring. It easily overrode Belle's orders, for they had been orders. It made her say to the old cook, 'Please, please, will you mind the children for me and make sure they don't get out. Please! I've got to go out and search—I've just got to!'

The old lady must have nodded; Aline had an idea she had wished her luck. She had the car out and was clumsily nosing it into the inferno of thick smoke. She was forcing down the panic that threatened to overwhelm her. Her eyes stung and her lungs were labouring for air. The sand whirled in a dervish's dance, beaten by the wind, which had suddenly turned.

Aline was not bush-wise enough to understand immediately what was happening, but then she saw the flames turn towards her and tried to back the car, which stalled. Into her mind flared small bits of information, seen on television, heard over the wireless, read in the newspapers. 'Don't leave your car, shelter in it.' But there were also those—some of the neighbours—who had spoken of the danger of igniting and exploding petrol. And sitting here would not help her to find Jill and Diane.

She stumbled out and turned towards the left lane, where there were no dancing devils of flames. Screams suddenly came to her ears—Jill's voice, and that of another child. And then she saw them, flat in one of those small 'lakes' and fortunately one where the dry had not sucked out all the water. There wasn't much fluid, but the children were lying in it, flat, the small discs of their faces only above the water. And then Aline was with them, her arms around them, admonishing them, 'Down, as far down as you can!' The water was in her mouth, foetid and yet saving. Branches crashed off trees, singed leaves whirled around, and then there was a crash and darkness descended heavily.

At first Aline did not know where she was or why she was there. She knew she did not have a head but a balloon, and that the balloon hurt. She slept and woke, and realised that the flitting shadows were nurses and that she had a ceiling above her and a mattress beneath, and that therefore she must be in hospital. She tried to ask why she was in hospital, but either the nurses could not hear or would not, because they only smiled reassuringly and rubbed slivers of ice across her lips. Aline gave up the unequal struggle and slept.

When she woke again, her sight was clear and she saw Glenn sitting beside her bed. His first words confirmed that—who but Glenn would greet a patient with, 'You outsize fool, you!'

She tried to smile at him, lovingly, and it did not seem to matter what had been between them. She tried to say something, but she could not get it out, and before she managed to clear her throat a nurse loomed up and ordered him out—a slim chit of a thing, ordering out the arrogant Glenn! Aline started to cry weakly and Nurse wanted to know where it hurt and if she would only swallow 'this' she would be all right.

'Sick of drugs. *No*,' said Aline.

Funnily enough the nurse did not seem to mind. She said, 'Good girl,' and wiped away the tears and did not make her drink the cloudy something in the small glass.

As the time passed, Glenn came in again and again, but so often when he came there was Belle too, and Aline, in her feverish state, started to wonder in her heart, which ached more than her sore head, if it was not going to be Bill and Belle but Belle and Glenn.

True, Glenn had never shown any preference for the beautiful woman, but, Glenn being

Glenn, he was not likely to show his feelings. True too, he had saved the children's lives and hers as well.

Food tasted like sawdust, but it could not be the hospital's fault, because everybody else ate. The nights seemed endless, yet they could not be.

'I wish you'd go away and stop pestering me about signing papers regarding my legacy which I won't take,' snapped Aline at Bill. 'You're talking and talking and you're making my head ache! Why don't you take Jill and the twins and Belle and go away for a holiday? It would get me some peace and quiet, and you'd be out of my hair.'

To her surprise Bill flushed scarlet. 'Aline, I mean . . . I hope you don't mind?'

'Mind what?' asked the girl tiredly.

'Well, you know, you and me. But Belle and I . . . Well, you know it wasn't really serious between us. You said so yourself.'

Pleasure drove strength into the weak voice. 'Do you mean, Bill, that you and Belle are serious? Oh, how wonderful!' The weak tears ran down her face.

'Get the hell out of here,' said Glenn, suddenly appearing at her bedside. 'Haven't you any sense at all, Bill?'

Now there was silence in the small ward, a silence that was unbroken by the rainclouds which chased the last traces of smoke and smudges out of the air. Then a bird started to sing into the gloom and some flowers which had somehow survived bravely flaunted their colours against the sky.

'I didn't know you loved Bill,' said Glenn. 'I ought to have seen it. But I was so—so busy talking myself out of believing Mrs Delamaine and not succeeding, when I ought to have seen that she just wanted me for Marlene and nobody was and would be allowed to compete. Don't cry, Aline.'

A golden shaft of happiness cleared the last trace of worry from Aline's mind. She turned to him, eyes shining above her bandages, mouth tender in her small face, and borrowed a leaf from his own book.

'You fool, Glenn,' she smiled. 'I don't love Jim. I don't love Bill. I never have. I only love you.'

And then she was in his arms. For a long time there was silence between them. Then shyly, she broke the silence. 'Is this Lesson Number Three, Glenn?' she asked.

For a moment he tore himself apart from her. 'It's going to be a never-ending lesson,' he said.

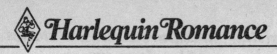

Harlequin Romance

Coming Next Month

2923 THERE MUST BE LOVE Samantha Day
Marriage, a home, children—that's what Vanessa, a school librarian, dreams of. So how could she let herself fall for Shane, a famous writer and reputed ladies' man? He's certainly not the marrying kind.

2924 MAN OF IRON Catherine George
When her adoptive mother dies, Antonia is surprised to learn her real mother has always kept watch over her and wants her to come to Brazil. Only the arrogant Jaime de Almeida dampens her spirits. He suspects Antonia's motives!

2925 IMPOSSIBLE TO FORGET Sally Heywood
Claudia, trying to get a hotel chain to franchise her beauty clinics, is shocked to find the top man is Daniel Sinnington. He seems to have completely forgotten their teenage love affair and his abrupt desertion. For Claudia, her son is a permanent reminder....

2926 TARIK'S MOUNTAIN Dana James
Laura's posting to Gibraltar is a real career boost. Yet, given the job of escorting sharp-minded journalist Brent Lewis around the project, she finds that against his irresistible attraction, her professional integrity is in danger of being compromised.

2927 A GOLDEN TOUCH Mary Moore
In Vashti's experience, men aren't to be trusted. Head, not heart, and a modern computer, is the way to go in seriously choosing a husband she'd swap for her high-flying career. Actually, as it turns out, the choice isn't that simple....

2928 FORTUNES OF LOVE Jessica Steele
Eden will do anything for her loved stepbrother, Thomas, her only family now. So when Thomas wants to marry Sterne Parnell's young ward, Eden aids and abets the young couple. Facing up afterward to a man like Sterne is another matter!

Available in August wherever paperback books are sold, or through Harlequin Reader Service:

In the U.S.
901 Fuhrmann Blvd.
P.O. Box 1397
Buffalo, N.Y. 14240-1397

In Canada
P.O. Box 603
Fort Erie, Ontario
L2A 5X3

**Exciting, adventurous, sensual stories
of love long ago**

On Sale Now:

SATAN'S ANGEL by Kristin James

Slater was the law in a land that was as wild and untamed as he was himself, but all that changed when he met Victoria Stafford. She had been raised to be a lady, but that didn't mean she had no will of her own. Their search for her kidnapped cousin brought them together, but they were too much alike for the course of true love to run smooth.

PRIVATE TREATY by Kathleen Eagle

When Jacob Black Hawk rescued schoolteacher Carolina Hammond from a furious thunderstorm, he swept her off her feet in every sense of the word, and she knew that he was the only man who would ever make her feel that way. But society had put barriers between them that only the most powerful and overwhelming love could overcome...

Look for them wherever Harlequin books are sold.

PAMELA BROWNING

...is fireworks on the green at the Fourth of July and prayers said around the Thanksgiving table. It is the dream of freedom realized in thousands of small towns across this great nation.

But mostly, the Heartland is its people. People who care about and help one another. People who cherish traditional values and give to their children the greatest gift, the gift of love.

American Romance presents HEARTLAND, an emotional trilogy about people whose memories, hopes and dreams are bound up in the acres they farm.

HEARTLAND...the story of America.

Don't miss these heartfelt stories: American Romance #237 SIMPLE GIFTS (March), #241 FLY AWAY (April), and #245 HARVEST HOME (May).

HRT-1

Coming in April

Harlequin Category Romance Specials!

Look for six new and exciting titles from this mix of two genres.

4 Regencies—lighthearted romances set in England's Regency period (1811-1820)

2 Gothics—romance plus suspense, drama and adventure

Regencies

Daughters Four by Dixie Lee McKeone
She set out to matchmake for her sister, but reckoned without the Earl of Beresford's devilish sense of humor.

Contrary Lovers by Clarice Peters
A secret marriage contract bound her to the most interfering man she'd ever met!

Miss Dalrymple's Virtue by Margaret Westhaven
She needed a wealthy patron—and set out to buy one with the only thing she had of value....

The Parson's Pleasure by Patricia Wynn
Fate was cruel, showing her the ideal man, then making it impossible for her to have him....

Gothics

Shadow over Bright Star by Irene M. Pascoe
Did he want her shares to the silver mine, her love—or her life?

Secret at Orient Point by Patricia Werner
They seemed destined for tragedy despite the attraction between them....

CAT88A-1

**If *YOU* enjoyed this book,
your daughter may enjoy**

Romances from

CROSSWINDS

Keepsake is a series of tender, funny, down-to-earth romances for younger teens.

The simple boy-meets-girl romances have lively and believable characters, lots of action and romantic situations with which teens can identify.

Available now wherever books are sold.

ADULT-1

HARLEQUIN SIGNATURE EDITION

Penny Jordan

Stronger than Yearning

He was the man of her dreams!

The same dark hair, the same mocking eyes; it was as if the Regency rake of the portrait, the seducer of Jenna's dream, had come to life. Jenna, believing the last of the Deverils dead, was determined to buy the great old Yorkshire Hall—to claim it for her daughter, Lucy, and put to rest some of the painful memories of Lucy's birth. She had no way of knowing that a direct descendant of the black sheep Deveril even existed—or that James Allingham and his own powerful yearnings would disrupt her plan entirely.

Penny Jordan's first Harlequin Signature Edition *Love's Choices* was an outstanding success. Penny Jordan has written more than 40 best-selling titles—more than 4 million copies sold.

Now, be sure to buy her latest bestseller, *Stronger Than Yearning*. Available wherever paperbacks are sold—in June.

STRONG-1R